The Flight
The Phantom
Tamanrasset

Simon Weipert

The Flight
The Phantom
Tamanrasset

© 2013 Simon Weipert
Layout, cover design, printing and publication: BoD – Books on Demand, Norderstedt, Germany
ISBN: 978-3-7322-7095-8

Content

THE FLIGHT	7
THE PHANTOM	68
TAMANRASSET	97

THE FLIGHT

The vast, dark blue expanses of the Atlantic Ocean stretched deeply below her. At this high altitude, even the clouds resembled a delicate netting which almost merged with the surface of the water and whose shadows barely contrasted with it. Her eyes wandered to the North American continent and the coast of Florida on the left, where their voyage had begun two days ago. She was able to distinguish the coastline clearly, which evoked images of the subtropical landscape surrounding the space center. She was sure that she could feel the warmth and the moisture on her skin, the rushing of the sea, the soft breeze of the night, and the chirping of the crickets. She remembered her first ride to the Cape and her expectations before her first space flight, her joy, her enthusiasm, and the feeling that she was entering the world of her dreams. While the Earth continued rotating, more distant images emerged in her thoughts: Memories of her childhood in a suburb of Columbia in South Carolina arose in her mind, the park-like landscape full of trees, gardens, and houses where she had grown up as well as the home of her parents and the piano music of her youth.

Dusk was falling in Europe, and the east of the continent was fusing with the dark of the night. In the west, however, the last sun rays were still illuminating the places where she had spent many years and aroused the memories of her time in Germany. Images and impressions appeared in her mind and for a moment revived this close and nonetheless so distant world.

While the spaceship was moving towards darkness, her short break was coming to an end and it was time for her to return to the rest of the crew, which was preparing for the long flight through space.

The two other astronauts were already waiting for Catherine: James, the captain, who would fly the spaceship on its way to Mars and back, and co-pilot David, who, like her, was also responsible for the experiments as a mission specialist. In an hour they would leave the Earth´s orbit and begin their voyage to the Red Planet. The spaceship consisted of a space shuttle for landing on the remote planet and returning to Earth and a three-stage propulsion unit, of which two stages were needed for the flight to Mars. The third stage of the propulsion unit was intended to remain in orbit around Mars and be used for the return flight. The space shuttle, which was built like a vertical take-off aircraft, would land on Mars and later return to Earth, where it was to land like a normal passenger airplane. In comparison with spaceships of earlier generations, the "Constellation" shuttle offered ample space. In addition to the cockpit, it included a room for scientific experiments, a team room, and three bedrooms for the astronauts, as well as a small greenhouse, which supplied the crew with fresh food during their long absence from Earth. Thanks to progress in the creation of artificial gravity, the astronauts were able to move on board the space shuttle almost like they did on Earth. Although there had been two flights to Mars before, the third one still managed to capture the interest of people worldwide; however, its effect was not as great as during the first mission five years ago. At that time, the expectations and, above all, the hope to find traces of life on Mars had been very high. So far, they had not materialized, but since only a small part of the planet had been explored so far, Catherine, like everyone else, dreamed of being the first researcher to make such a discovery. She felt this fascination more strongly than the tension that was mounting inside of her before this first long space flight following some short trips to the space station which she had previously made. No great difficulties had arisen during the previous two flights although the journeys through space, which took many months, were still at the limit of technology. Nevertheless, Catherine asked herself what it would be like to live together with two other people in a very confined space for two years without any possibility of going back.

She washed her hands, combed her short hair, and had a brief look into the mirror before she returned to James and David. Catherine was considerably smaller and more delicate than the two other astronauts, and her dark brown, almost black hair and brown eyes formed a charming contrast with the light blue of her spacesuit.

"There you are," said James. "I already thought that you had fallen asleep."

"No, I'm fully awake and all set for the great journey."

James went to the pilot's seat and crammed himself into it. He was tall and strongly built, and his blue eyes and black hair along with his sharp facial features gave his face a distinctive expression.

David was already sitting in the co-pilot's seat. He was slightly smaller than James, had dark-blonde hair and brown eyes, and his face appeared younger than one would have expected for someone at the age of 35.

Catherine sat down at her place behind David, and the three astronauts began working on the tasks to be completed before their departure. David took care of the radio communications, James checked the displays and instruments and undertook some small last-minute changes following the instructions of the ground control station, while Catherine went through the list of instruments and made sure that everything was prepared for the flight to Mars.

Nervousness was starting to set in even though all three hid their emotions well. Their movements and their voices demonstrated a strong familiarity with the routine as they completed the tasks which they had practiced so many times before during their training. However, this time something was different from the flights to the space station, which all three astronauts had already experienced. Even though the mix of exhilaration and subliminal fear was well known to them, Catherine in particular felt deeply agitated as if her soul had become a volcano which made her feel all the depths of her existence.

The ground station informed them again that no solar eruptions were to be expected in the weeks and months to come according to the latest data and that they would not cross any meteoroid showers on their way to Mars. These predictions were constantly updated and part of the daily routine despite the fact that precise observations had been carried out before and the orbits of all asteroids and meteoroid swarms had been calculated.

"We shouldn´t encounter any unpleasant surprises during the first days," said James.

"Yes, everything looks good, but you never know exactly what´s going to happen," replied Catherine.

The last five minutes in orbit passed in an atmosphere of mounting tension. Their home planet, which showed them its night side, lay behind them, and before them extended the starry sky, which gave them an idea of the dimensions of space that they had never experienced on Earth. Catherine had the impression that infinity was opening before her and bundling all the hopes, dreams, and fears of her life.

When they finally heard the noise of the engines and felt the acceleration, all the tension began to dissolve and gave way to a feeling of ecstatic joy. First, they all contained their emotions, but eventually David said:

"The first step has been completed."

"Yes, now our journey can really begin," said James, and Catherine smiled, showing her relief.

As the Earth behind them became smaller and smaller and the glaring sunlight began to outshine their home planet, the spaceship made its way towards the point where Mars would be in five months.

After they had left the orbit around Earth, the astronauts resumed their individual duties. James controlled the flight, while Catherine and David once again discussed the experiments which they were supposed to carry out at the beginning. From the rear window of the space shuttle they saw the Earth, which had already rotated further, and observed Europe, whose illuminated cities offered a magnificent view.

"We won´t enjoy this sight for a long time," said Catherine.

"I´ll miss it," answered David and added: "I´m going to call my family soon. This will make my farewell at least somewhat easier."

"Let´s go through the magnetosphere measurements again," said Catherine after a while, and they began to prepare for the observations.

After another two hours, the three astronauts met for dinner and planned their activities for the following days. Afterwards, the first break began for Catherine and David while James stayed awake in order to maintain contact with the ground station and to be able to take action in case any trouble arose.

Catherine and David went to their bedrooms, which offered enough space for a bed, a small window, and a closet. Catherine listened to some music and observed the starry sky, which from here looked much larger and more overwhelming than on

Earth. She followed the wide and nonetheless delicate ribbon of the Milky Way, which stretched from one side of the sky to the other and never seemed to end. She felt like a tiny grain of dust in an immense ocean of light and darkness. Once again, she became aware of her vulnerability in the infinity of space, but nevertheless she also felt deeply secure and part of this world of light and shade. When she finally lay down to sleep, half of her six-hour resting period had already passed.

After she had woken up from her short nap, she and David went into the cockpit in order to relieve James, who had been waiting for them and looked tired and tense.

"It´s about time," he said to David and Catherine when they entered the cockpit.

"I know, the last six hours must have been quite strenuous for you," replied David.

During their training, Catherine and David had noticed that James was sometimes slightly irritable, but these phases had always been short. 45 year old James was the oldest crew member and had been an air force officer before he had applied for the post of an astronaut. During his time in the air force, he had been stationed in Afghanistan, Iraq, and Kongo several times and had been involved in battles against insurgents with his unit. These experiences had left traces in his soul even though they were nothing uncommon for a soldier and had not been taken seriously by his superiors.

"I´m going to bed now. Make sure that the flight course remains within the permitted range of deviation."

"All right," said David. "Have there been any unusual occurrences?," he asked. "No, except for a very brief disruption of radio communications, probably due to slightly increased solar activity. According to the ground station, this is insignificant, though," James informed them and went to his cabin.

David wished him a good night, but James hardly heard what

he had said. As soon as he arrived in his cabin, he lay down and immediately fell into a deep sleep, which was sometimes interrupted by troubled dreams.

Meanwhile, Catherine and David completed the last preparations for the magnetospheric research experiments which were scheduled to be carried out soon. Along with some asteroid observations, these were the only scientific projects planned during the flight to Mars. The measurements were intended to begin in approximately five hours, and they would be completed after several days. Afterwards, a long period of waiting would begin for the astronauts until the approach to Mars. Everyone had made plans for this time. All of them had stored hundreds of books on their personal readers and James and David had brought some computer games, while Catherine had almost her entire music collection with her. Although astronauts had often complained about boredom during past flights and had sometimes considered it a heavy burden, Catherine was hardly concerned about it because she knew that her ability to drift away into her dreams and the world of her soul would make her long absence from Earth easier.

After they had finished their preparations, David and Catherine worked out on their treadmills for one hour. This was also part of the daily routine in order to prevent muscle loss. After James had woken up, they met for dinner.

"Did you recover somewhat?," asked David.

"Yes, I´m all right. I slept quite well even though I sometimes felt slightly uneasy," answered James.

"That´s not unusual during such a flight," said Catherine. "Over time, everything will become routine, and then we´ll all sleep better."

After the short break, the three astronauts resumed their tasks. Catherine and David began with the magnetosphere measurements, while James fulfilled his duties as a pilot. Growing distance slowly began to affect the radio communication with Earth, which meant having to wait longer for an answer during a conversation. Currently, the delay was only several seconds, but it would increase to approximately 25 minutes by the time they arrived on Mars.

After the last measurements and experiments had been completed during the following days, the long period of waiting began. The three astronauts spent their free time not only reading books, but they also often spoke in detail about their expectations and experiences. Moreover, their resting periods had been prolonged from six to eight hours. Catherine used this time not only to sleep, but she also often enjoyed the view of the star-filled sky. Once, her eyes wandered back to Earth, which could still be distinguished as a small dot from afar and she wondered what was going on there. She had talked to her father and her sister in South Carolina three days ago and had told them about her first days on board the spaceship. Still, she did not have much time for this conversation because each crew member only had 10 minutes per week for personal telephone calls. Her father had just returned from his medical practice, and her sister Anne was working on her thesis and was excited about graduating from college. She was 28 years old, five years younger than Catherine. Both had grown up together in South Carolina before Catherine spent several years in Germany, where her grandfather had come from before he emigrated to America.

Catherine´s thoughts wandered back further into her childhood and to her first memories.

She saw her parents´ house on a small hill in a suburb of Columbia, surrounded by firs and broad-leaved trees. It was an older, two-storey wood house from the 1930s with a long driveway and stone steps leading up to the front door. There was a porch in the back overlooking a large yard with a lush green lawn and several groups of tall trees, where Catherine had often spent her time with her sister as a child. The living room afforded a view of this peaceful oasis. A black grand piano stood next to the fireplace, on which she and her parents had played every day. Both her father and her mother loved classical music, and the melodies emerging from the wonderful heirloom instrument formed some of her fondest memories. As a child, she listened to her parents for hours lost in a world of daydreams.

It was also during her young years that she developed a growing interest in mathematics and science. Especially the nightly sky with its millions of stars deeply fascinated her. Sometimes she got up, turned the light off, and observed the infinite black sky which was dotted with numerous points of light of different sizes. She wondered how far away they were. Her astronomy books gave her a vague idea of the dimensions of the universe, and since her father had also been captivated by the world of the stars as a child, he was able to answer many of her questions.

When she was seven years old, Catherine began to play the piano herself and was first taught by her mother, who had studied music in New York. She still well remembered the first small melodies, her feelings when she touched the keys, the smell of the wood, and the warmth of the fireplace in the winter. At first, she spent half an hour playing the piano every day and took great delight in the sound of music even though she sometimes found practicing difficult. Later, when she was a teenager, the instrument gradually became a companion, and she often played for hours at night and on the weekend as though she were having a dialogue with herself and the music. Anne also loved to listen to her as did her friends and schoolmates, who were deeply impressed by her musical ability. Her mother had often dreamed that she would become a pianist and tried to rouse her ambition, but Catherine did not consider music as a profession, but rather as a place where her imagination had no boundaries and was free. German was another great passion of hers at that time. She spent hours learning the language and thought about getting to know Europe and her grandfather's home country later on.

Nevertheless, she also pursued her scientific interests, and by the time she finished high school she had made up her mind to become a mathematician or a physicist. When she told her parents that she wanted to study physics in Germany, her father supported her, but it was difficult for her mother, who did not want to abandon her goal of making Catherine a concert pianist so easily. Around this time, she began to question the Christian faith of her parents she was brought up in at home. Could something like a sphere beyond the visible world really exist? Her immersion in the natural sciences made her doubt it more and more. If the question were considered rationally, all scientific facts spoke against the existence of a soul which was independent from the body and lived on after death. How was this compatible with the idea of an afterlife? Nonetheless, she never wanted to entirely exclude that rational thinking was only one form of cognition and that her daydreams might also contain a core of truth. These dreams told her that the existence of a world beyond the material sphere was no absurd idea. Especially when she observed the starry sky, she often felt as though she were part of a world which did not end at its material limits.

Her parents were divided concerning her doubts about conventional belief. While her father confessed that he had very similar ideas, her mother showed little understanding for her daughter, who also in this respect was venturing down entirely different paths than herself. At that time, Catherine felt more sure than ever that it was time for her to leave Columbia and to go her own way, and also her parents sensed after the arguments of the past months that it would be the best for her if a new phase of her life began.

In the summer of the same year, she flew to Frankfurt. It was the first time that she saw the country where her grandfather had spent his youth. She had embarked on this first great journey of her life feeling both a sense of melancholy about leaving her parents' house and joy about all the new things she would experience. When the airplane took off, she felt that she was leaving part of herself behind and that the unknown was beginning to replace the old. During the night, while most of the other passengers were sleeping, she opened the blind of her window and looked outside. It was a new moon night, and the stars were clearly visible in the darkness of the night sky. The airplane seemed to move above infinite chains of clouds shaped like an endless mountain range, above which time and distance lost their importance. Beyond this surreal landscape stretched the vastness of the night sky, whose constellations Catherine knew so well. Even though she was aware that these stars were inaccessibly distant, they appeared to her like a familiar part of her inner world and gave her a feeling of great security. When dawn broke and the airplane approached its destination, she felt that she had left her childhood and her youth behind her and that she was ready for what was going to come.

At first glance, Frankfurt reminded her of an American city and thus gave her the impression that she had found a new home right away. When she began to attend her first lectures in physics at the university after several weeks, she had already become used to life in Germany, and she had also improved her German such that she was able to express herself fluently in the language. Nevertheless, she did not entirely blend into daily life in the new country as she had become close friends with another American physics student during a language class. Roger shared her passion for science and in particular her fascination with the world of the stars. Over the course of the next few months, they became a couple and finally moved into an apartment together in the section of the city where Catherine lived. During the three years they spent together, they went on several trips to southern Germany, Italy and France. The Black Forest and the Alps were the first regions which she got to know in Germany. She still well remembered her trip to Freiburg that fall. She fondly recalled the charming city and in particular her ride to the top of the mountains of the Black Forest when the thick fog disappeared in the light of the rising sun and the clear air revealed a distant view from the Swiss Alps and Montblanc to the Vosges, while the gray sea of fog covered the world beneath them.

Catherine had continued to play the piano whenever she had some free time. Roger often listened to her for what seemed like hours, spellbound by the passion that rose from the instrument. Even if he did not play an instrument himself, he nevertheless began to share her enthusiasm for music. It was during this time that they began to make plans for their future together. They thought they would return to America in the hope of finding jobs at a university and then start a family although Catherine still was not sure whether a family would hinder her career plans. From time to time, she and Roger had even had arguments over this issue.

In the spring of her last year at the university, Roger went to Karlsruhe to visit a close friend for a few days. They had said goodbye as always, and Catherine had gone downtown afterwards. Two days later, while she was working at her desk at home, the doorbell rang. She jumped and when she went downstairs two police officers were standing at the door. With one look she could see that they seemed uneasy about the task at hand. Catherine sensed immediately that something was wrong and deep down already knew what it was.

When she opened the door, one of the police officers said:

"Ms. Weaver, we are very sorry, but we are here to inform you that Mr. Williams died in a traffic accident two hours ago. He was on the interstate when the vehicle in front of him braked suddenly. His car started to skid and crashed into a tree. Unfortunately, the emergency physician was not able to save his life."

Inside of her, life came to a standstill, as though she were torn between a dream and reality. Only after the police officers had left did the agonizing reality hit her and push all other thoughts into the background. Despair overwhelmed her and paralyzed her for hours, days, and nights as though a thick layer of ice had formed on her soul. It took several days before she was able to return to the university and call her parents, who tried to comfort her. Even after she had found her way back into a routine, many things remained different in her life. She began to ask the questions which had been on her mind before: Does anything remain after death? Is there a world beyond the material sphere? In the past, she had always been rather skeptical. Based on scientific insights, the soul with all its thoughts, feelings, and dreams could ultimately only be a result of organic processes and, hence, part of the physical world. Even now, her mind told her that there was no reason to doubt this scientific perspective. Nevertheless, she could not help feeling that Roger was still part of her life and somewhat mysteriously still there, and she began to ask herself whether dreams and intuition were not also part of reality and in their way also an element of knowledge. Although she struggled to distance herself from what had happened and was relieved to feel her strength slowly returning in the coming weeks, this question continued to occupy her thoughts, and despite all doubts she hesitantly began to answer it positively. Roger stayed with her, in her daydreams and in her music, and she no longer considered these dreams as mere illusion, but regarded them as part of her life.

Six months later, Catherine was awarded her degree and returned home. She had missed her parents and her sister even though she had visited them twice a year. She began working as a software developer with an airplane manufacturer in North Carolina and wrote her doctoral dissertation on the side. Although she had always had a strong work ethic, both during her school years and at the university, she now lived solely for her work, which earned her satisfaction and recognition. After a while, she was assigned the development of computer programs for space projects, which rekindled her interest in astronomy. Two years later, she saw an advertisement declaring that positions for astronauts were vacant, and after some consideration she decided to apply even though she deemed it unlikely that she would really be hired. Much to her surprise, however, she was invited to a job interview. The sudden possibility that her dream might come true spurred her on to do all she could to make it happen. In the evening and at night, she spent hours searching for every piece of available information on planned space flights and potential flights to Mars. With each passing day, her enthusiasm for space research continued to grow. When she finally received the news that she had been selected as one of several thousand applicants, she felt a strong conviction that she was doing the right thing even though she was aware of the dangers of space flights and even though her parents and her sister had sometimes cautioned her despite their admiration for her determination and her enthusiasm.

During her training as an astronaut and the preparation for her first flight, Catherine was so busy with her work that she hardly had any time for music. But when she did play, she abandoned herself to her thoughts and dreams. Like before, images from the past and the future appeared in her mind, and Roger also lived on in these images and with him the feeling of security in a world which did not end at the limits of the material sphere.

About one year after she had completed her training, Catherine went on her first space flight. She still well remembered the lift-off of the space shuttle, her stay at the space station, and her first view of the Earth from above. At the same time the first manned flights to Mars were being planned, something that had been in the making for many decades. Although almost all unmanned probes meanwhile reached their destination, the awareness of the dangers inherent in such a mission and the consequences that would have to be borne in the event of a failure during a manned flight to Mars were two things that remained ever present in the minds of all those involved. Despite some minor difficulties, however, the first two manned flights were a great success and fascinated the public and the media worldwide. As during the moon landings long ago, man's first step on Mars was celebrated as a big step in the history of mankind. Afterwards, engineers, physicians, and psychologists all tried to gain knowledge from these first flights. Despite many long-term trials prior to these missions it had been unclear how the astronauts would fare during such a long flight and how they would cope with it mentally. During the first two flights, however, all had gone well also in this respect despite occasional arguments and some short phases of depression some crew members had suffered through. The experience of numerous past space flights had also clearly shown that it helped the social climate if at least one woman was on board the spacecraft. This insight had again been strongly confirmed during the first flights to Mars. This was one of the reasons why Catherine was proposed for the third flight, especially since it was believed that due to her rather quiet personality she could play an important role in the social structure of the crew particularly during such a long flight.

When Catherine heard that she would fly to Mars, she was

ecstatic. For her, this meant the realization of a dream that she had entertained since her childhood, a dream she had hardly believed would come true even at the beginning of her astronaut career. When the training for the flight began, she immersed herself completely in her work and often spent the entire day and the weekends preparing experiments and studying the conditions on Mars. Right from the start, she had established a good relationship with the other two astronauts on the mission and believed that she would be able to manage quite well on the long journey to Mars with them. She quickly developed a strong liking for David, and she was also able to become friends with James especially since she felt that he had also experienced some difficulties in his life. The last months and weeks preceding their flight seemed to pass faster and faster the closer the time of departure came. Still, somehow, when the "Constellation" finally lifted off, time almost seemed to stand still as if it wanted to let the astronauts and the world feel the extraordinary character of this moment. Hundreds of thousands of spectators had come to follow the lift-off with their own eyes, but in their thoughts the astronauts were already in space on the way to a distant world and were almost oblivious to what was happening on Earth. When they finally arrived in orbit, they became even more aware that this was not the goal of their voyage, but only the starting point of a long journey.

All these memories and thoughts went through Catherine's mind during this long resting period while the spaceship was traversing the immense expanses of space and the Earth was gradually disappearing into the darkness. During the flight from the Earth orbit to Mars, one astronaut was responsible for flight control while another could enjoy some free time or prepare for the exploration of the still vastly mysterious planet and the third one slept in his cabin. Since the flight was largely automatically controlled and radio communications required only little attention, some time remained for more personal conversations. David and Catherine got to know each other much better and learned a lot about each other's lives. Sometimes James also gave the others a tiny glimpse into his soul, although for the most part he remained very reserved. Once, he told his counterparts how several of his comrades were killed during an attack on an airbase.

"The attackers ambushed us. They emerged from nowhere and began to fire at us with sub-machine guns. We tried to find shelter, but the enemy seemed to be attacking us from all sides. We had to defend ourselves and got involved in a battle which lasted several hours. I was lucky and wasn't hit, but two of my comrades suffered head injuries and died at the scene of the attack. Three other soldiers from our unit were severely wounded by shots and flying shrapnel. They were screaming in pain, but we weren't able to help them. Again and again, we came under heavy fire, and the enemy soldiers would reappear suddenly like out of the middle of nowhere and shoot at us. After a while, we were finally able to ward off the attack and retreat, but I'll never be able to forget those hours and the sight of my dead and injured comrades."

David and Catherine were visibly moved and tried to express their sympathy, but their conversation was soon interrupted by radio communications with the ground station. Immediately afterwards, it was time for James' resting period and David and Catherine remained alone. After completing all their tasks, they continued their conversation and talked about their youth and school time. David came from Colorado and had two sisters, Rachel and Edith, who had died of leukemia as a young woman.

"As children, we had lots of fun together. We used to play ball for hours in the yard behind the house. When we got older, Rachel and Edith often went jogging with me, or we went on long bike tours through the mountains, from which we sometimes returned late at night. Rachel´s interest was in literature and languages, while Edith drew really well and wanted to become a designer. I was the scientist in our family and took after my father, who was a civil engineer. Soon after I had started studying electrical engineering, Edith began developing more frequent infections and slowly became weaker and shorter of breath even though she had been so athletic before. We went to the doctor, who sent her to a hospital and prepared us for the possibility that she might have leukemia. Deep down we hoped that he was wrong, but he wasn´t. Worse, we were told that the prognosis wasn´t very good. Nonetheless, Edith took this devastating and depressing news with an amazing calmness and thus helped all of us to cope with the initial shock and our despair. Even though she had never been religious like most of our other family members, she didn´t seem to be afraid of death. Instead, she was convinced that the dead and the living were part of a comprehensive community and that a fragment of us remained after death. This idea seemed strange to us because before, we had actually always believed that life was over when a person was biologically dead. The notion of a world beyond seemed absurd. Still, Edith´s growing conviction in the face of death made us doubt our beliefs, and we didn´t want to exclude this possibility entirely despite our initial misgivings. After her death, we sometimes felt that she was still there with us and part of our family. This feeling in me kept growing stronger and stronger, and eventually it didn´t seem irrational any more. It made sense to me even though I couldn´t really explain it. Around that time, I developed a real passion for long-distance running. Every time I was out there I´d start daydreaming, something I had never done much of in the past since it had always seemed so pointless. You know, something that only poets do, but certainly not scientists. In these dreams I could feel that Edith was there, and just as she had I also started to see myself as just one little piece in a very big puzzle. Sometimes, I even get this feeling here in space when I'm observing the stars and looking at the Earth."

"For me, it's the same," said Catherine and told him about Roger and her own daydreams. "Of course, I'm familiar with the rational explanations for these feelings and phenomena, but more and more I'm starting to believe that there might be something besides these explanations."

As they continued their flight to Mars, David and Catherine discovered that they had very many things in common and began spending as much time together as the schedule on board the spaceship permitted.

Despite the fact that they had been gone from Earth for quite a while, the atmosphere among the astronauts was still good. James was the only one who occasionally seemed to have a hard time coping. At times he looked slightly depressed after his breaks. He often had nightmares during which he relived his wartime episodes in the darkness of his cabin. Once he recalled a combat scene so vividly in a dream that it was as though it had happened in real life. He was on an air base in the desert like the one he had been on as a soldier. Fighter planes were dropping explosive and incendiary bombs, when suddenly enemy soldiers and guerrilla fighters attacked his unit. He heard the explosions and the screaming of the wounded and saw the disfigured corpses, some of which were burnt beyond recognition. A huge tank was moving towards him, threatening to crush both him and his comrades. When the armored vehicle was only a few yards away from them, he woke up drenched in sweat. He got dressed immediately even though his break was actually still far from over and sat on his bed for almost an entire hour, unable to free himself from his depressing thoughts and convinced that his nightmare would probably haunt him for hours. Finally he got up and began to read, but he was unable to concentrate and his mind kept drifting back to the battlefield. When his break ended after several hours, he returned to Catherine and David who noticed that he had slept badly.

"Were you having nightmares again?," Catherine asked him. James told her and David about his dream, albeit with some reluctance at first and David asked him about his career and his experiences in the air force. Although the military had drilled him that there was no place for emotions in the life of a soldier, James felt that perhaps the time had come to talk about his past.

"From the time I was a little boy, I absolutely wanted to become a pilot. Since my parents didn't have any money for expensive vocational training, I decided to join the air force as a career soldier for 10 years. After basic training, I learned to fly all kinds of different airplanes, just like I had imagined. Afterwards, I participated in several missions and wars around the world - in different Arab countries, in Afghanistan, and on aircraft carriers. I was also stationed in Congo with my unit. It was our task to end a civil war there and to pacify the country as it was officially called. In reality, however, one could hardly call it peace. I saw the impact of our attacks in satellite images, which showed streets and bridges, villages and dams that had been completely destroyed. I began to have doubts about my work, which became more severe over time. Then I was sent to the Arab desert with my squadron. During a combat mission against insurgents, I went through the hell which I relive incessantly in the worst of my nightmares. Sure, we were offered psychological help afterwards in order to try to cope with it all, but I can't say it really helped because most of us kept 'functioning' outwardly without really overcoming what had happened. Over time, the memories faded slightly, and the nightmares became less frequent. However, I had a second war experience several years later which prompted me not to extend my contract with the air force even though it was not quite as traumatic as the first one. At that time, I witnessed the consequences of a suicide attack in Afghanistan, during which several civilians and two of our men were injured. I didn´t see the actual explosion, but I saw people wounded and bleeding and others screaming in despair who ran away from the place of the attack. The whole incident brought back memories of the past and the nightmares began again. I asked myself how we were supposed to establish peace in a country where such terrorist attacks still occurred almost every day even after decades. All this finally made me decide to opt for a civil career after my 10-year contract with the air force had expired. Since I still loved flying, I began working as an airline pilot and studying electrical engineering in my free time until I heard that they were looking for astronauts one day. I decided to apply because the exploration of space had always fascinated me and I had also heard of the planned flights to Mars. My application was accepted thanks to my experiences and awards as a pilot. During the preparation for the flights, I gained more and more distance from my wartime experiences, and my nightmares also became rarer and rarer even though they never have disappeared entirely."

"Did you ever talk about these nightmares during this time?," asked Catherine.

"Yes, but nobody was really interested in them. I was only told that psychological tests had shown that I was very resistant to stress and that I had obviously coped well with my wartime experiences. During the first flights to the space station, I never had any problems though, even that one time when a retrorocket almost failed. This time, however, the long flight leaves a lot of time for us to confront our own personal issues, and this makes things somewhat different. But I´m sure that I´m going to make it."

"I´m also convinced of that," said David and added: "Such a flight is an entirely new experience for all of us and will change us greatly."

Three months had passed since their departure from Earth, and a large part of the voyage to Mars lay behind them. It would take another two months until they reached their destination. The routine on board the spaceship made it easier for the three astronauts to cope with the long journey in a confined space. It gave their days a fixed rhythm and thus also a sense of orientation during the seemingly endless flight without day and night. Nevertheless, they were aware every day of where they were and that they were moving farther and farther away from Earth, separated from the void by only a few inches. All six astronauts who had flown to Mars before them also knew this ambivalent feeling of fascination and subliminal fear. The closer they came to the Red Planet in the weeks to come, however, the more curiosity and the joy of being able to explore a new world prevailed. Even though a lot had been learned about the environment and the conditions on Mars during the first two manned flights and through numerous unmanned missions, many things remained obscure, and the sojourn of humans on the remote planet was still a risk. In addition to experiments for the determination of chemical compounds and the search for life from earlier periods, the tasks of the crew also included the exploration of a rather unfamiliar area, which had been mapped by satellites, but where no spacecraft had landed before. This region, which was not all too far from the volcano Olympus Mons, was well known because sandstorms and related phenomena were quite frequent there. Scientists had not yet been able to explain their causes precisely and they were intended to be researched in more depth during this expedition. All in all, the danger arising from them was considered to be rather low, as researchers believed that they did not pose any greater threat than similar storms on Earth. Nonetheless, the astronauts knew that they would travel on unknown terrain and therefore studied all the maps and satellite images carefully in order to be as familiar as possible with the conditions at the place of landing. It was planned that all three crew members would conduct experiments and explore the environment even though it was David and Catherine who were mainly responsible for the scientific research, while James was supposed to monitor the space shuttle and prepare the return flight later. In addition, he would take over part of the geological exploration and mapping of an area of approximately 200 square miles in size around the landing site. For these expeditions, the astronauts had two electrically driven all-terrain vehicles at their disposition. Precise knowledge of the terrain was particularly important because the three crew members would largely be left to their own devices due to the long transmission times of radio signals to Earth. Thus, during the last phase of the flight, they spent one to three hours every day preparing for the first days and weeks after landing.

Approximately 20 miles from the landing site, there was a rift valley system about 1,200 feet in depth, which they were intended to explore. Catherine, David, and James had sometimes asked themselves what would happen if one of them had an accident or were seriously injured. They had emergency equipment on board and all three of them had thoroughly studied all the measures to be taken in the event of an accident or illness during their training and preparation for the flight, but they knew that there was no solution and no way out in many cases. Faced with this reality, they frequently discussed all expeditions and potential difficulties in detail. It had been decided that James would take over the most dangerous part of terrain exploration, namely the expedition to the rift valley system because he had the most experience dealing with all-terrain vehicles under desert-like conditions. Catherine and David would examine the area around the landing site using the second, considerably smaller vehicle. All three astronauts had practiced driving both vehicles, but the conditions on Mars were difficult to imitate on Earth in simulations despite precise descriptions from the two previous missions. Their experiences had shown that vehicles handled differently and were harder to control on Mars in particular on fine sand due to weaker gravity. No serious accidents had occurred during the first two missions to the Red Planet, but it was necessary to review all driving techniques and strategies in depth since James would travel considerably farther away from the space shuttle and the steep inclines would make the terrain more demanding. In addition, the weather conditions and the likelihood of sand storms would pose further challenges.

However, they were still several weeks away from Mars, and the most difficult part of the entire flight to the Red Planet was still awaiting them: the landing phase. During landing, retrorockets decelerated the space shuttle, and shortly before touchdown the pilot responsible for the landing maneuver had to observe the terrain carefully and would have to take action if any problems occurred unexpectedly. James as well as David had studied this phase of the flight thoroughly during their preparation. Nevertheless, the final minutes remained a time of danger and uncertainty, which was always present in their minds even if they avoided talking about it.

Otherwise, the astronauts followed their daily routine, and living together on board the space shuttle proved to be easier than Catherine had imagined before departure. James was slightly tense and moody on some days, but after they had gotten to know him better, Catherine and David were able to understand how he must be feeling and accepted him the way he was. Catherine spent her free time either talking to David or listening to music in her cabin, which led her far away from the confined space of the shuttle in her dreams and thoughts. The closer they came to Mars, the more her feelings and thinking revolved around what was going to come. In her dreams, Catherine saw the world they would soon set foot in and the landscapes which had lost nothing of their exoticism and fascination despite all preparation. At the same time, however, she became more and more aware of how large the distance from the security of her home on Earth had become. Telephone conversations with her family had meanwhile become virtually impossible due to the long transmission time needed for the radio signals. The only way for her to communicate with her parents and her sister was through e-mails, which she sent every two to three days. Sometimes, she talked to David about the coming months on Mars and the separation from home. David shared her feelings and she knew that he felt the distance from Earth even more clearly than she did.

"I often feel lost in this infinite space," he had once said.

"Me too," answered Catherine, "but we are still part of one single world even if we are far away from home. And maybe whatever happens makes sense even if we don´t realize it right away. Sometimes I think that there is a kind of thread that runs through our life and leaves a trace which often only becomes apparent when we look back."

"I think you are right. I had a similar feeling when I faced the death of my sister, which seemed absurd at first glance. Here in space, so far from life on Earth, this feeling is particularly pronounced. I often have the impression that the death of my sister opened my eyes for what actually matters and was one of the reasons why I did what I wanted to do."

"Roger´s accident changed my life as well. Without this blow of fate, which seemed so meaningless at first, I might never have become an astronaut," answered Catherine. When she looked out of the window, she saw Mars so close for the first time that she was able to distinguish the surface of the planet even though it still appeared blurred.

"We're approaching our goal," she said.

The view of Mars became more fascinating every day. Even with the naked eye, they were able to discern more of the landscape which they had previously seen and read about only in books, images, and reports. As could be determined by the rather small northern polar cap, it was summer in the northern hemisphere of Mars, which also meant that it was quite warm with temperatures around freezing. This season as well as the landing site near the equator had been chosen deliberately because the rather mild temperatures were intended to facilitate the work of the crew. Approximately one week before landing, the place where the space shuttle would touch down was already clearly visible. It was located in a hilly region southeast of the volcano Olympus Mons, which dwarfed all other mountains, valleys, and canyons. Even from afar, the largest volcano of the solar system looked like a relic from the distant past. It stimulated the imagination of all astronauts who saw it and gave them a vague impression of what majestic landscapes may exist on other, much farther planets.

A few days before landing, excitement on board the space shuttle began to grow. James and David prepared intensively for all landing maneuvers and carefully studied the weather data transmitted daily via satellites. For the planned landing day, good weather and clear visibility were forecast, and the wind was expected to be weak. This would facilitate the control of the space shuttle on its descent through the atmosphere and during landing. Nevertheless, a certain anxiety filled all three astronauts in anticipation of one of the greatest conceivable experiences, namely of being one of the first people to set foot on the surface of another planet.

Several hours before the big moment, all astronauts were strapped into their seats and waiting for the space shuttle to decelerate and to orbit Mars. From a close distance, the two Mars moons Phobos and Deimos, which moved around the planet at different altitudes, were now clearly distinguishable. When they passed in front of Mars, even the craters and rift valleys on their surface were visible. As soon as the space shuttle had come close enough to the planet, James ignited the engines, which decelerated the spaceship such that it began to move in an orbit around Mars within a short time. The astronauts breathed a sigh of relief and were glad that this first important maneuver had been completed without problems. The space shuttle would now circle around the Red Planet for approximately 15 hours before the actual landing began. While they were orbiting Mars, the third propulsion stage, which they would need in order to return to Earth, was detached. The period in orbit not only gave them time to prepare for landing, but also allowed them to have a final rest. During their breaks, however, none of them wanted to miss the view of Mars, whose surface they passed at an altitude of about 200 miles. Catherine was enthraled by the interplay of light and shadow above the mountains and ravines, the craters of the volcanoes, and the white of the polar caps. She became aware of what a miracle it was that she was able to see another planet at close range. In her thoughts, she reflected on her life to date and her flight to Mars and almost had the impression that the journey which had led her here was not just the result of mere chance and arbitrary human decisions.

After just a few hours of sleep, all three astronauts met again in order to discuss the last details of the landing. They received the latest weather forecasts and reports on when and where turbulence had to be expected, which could be quite strong due to the high wind speeds on Mars. Shortly afterwards, the engines decelerated the space shuttle again, and the descent through the atmosphere, which covered the planet like a thin, red veil, began. The "Constellation" entered the atmosphere on the night side so that not much of the surface was visible at first. While they were flying towards the sun and the day, however, the reddish glow of the atmosphere gradually became stronger, and the breaking dawn provided a view of the landscapes which they were approaching. The sunrise reminded Catherine of her flights on Earth, but nonetheless the view caused her to lose herself more and more in this new, different world. They were still several thousand miles away from the landing site, and the mountains, valleys, and canyons were passing quickly beneath them when suddenly the space shuttle got caught in heavy turbulence in the denser layers of the atmosphere. It was stronger than expected. Despite all preparation and the reports of previous crews, the three astronauts experienced a feeling of deep-seated fear, and Catherine was clenching her fists even though she tried not to appear anxious. As the turbulence became even more violent, James was hardly able to keep the space shuttle on course using the vernier engines. After several minutes, which felt like eternity to the astronauts, they reached calmer layers of the atmosphere, and the tension abated. Their speed was still high as they approached the planned landing site, which was more than 700 miles away. Olympus Mons appeared on the horizon, and they were able to see the mountain in its entirety from this distance. This sight surpassed all their expectations. The mountain was as big as an entire mountain range on Earth. Its summit rose above the altitude at which they were now, and its slopes extended over hundreds of miles into the surrounding plains. As they came closer, they were only able to glimpse part of the immense mountain, but nevertheless they had the impression that they were flying by its slopes and cliffs even though James kept a distance of at least 45 miles. Directly beneath the space shuttle a steep slope dropped several miles separating the volcano from the plain, where rift valleys and impact craters became more clearly discernible. At the same time, the three smaller volcanoes Ascraeus Mons, Pavonis Mons, and Arsia Mons, which also rose many miles above the plains around them, appeared more distinctly on the horizon. Even the smallest one was far bigger than any mountain on Earth. While Catherine was held spellbound by the panorama, the space shuttle decelerated further, and the immediate preparation for landing began. As they approached the surface of the planet, what was visible of Olympus Mons became smaller and smaller. This made the enormous size of the volcano even more apparent. From the lower altitude, the spacecraft looked like a tiny, fragile artefact next to the bare and towering rocky cliffs of the gigantic mountain. As they came closer to the landing site, the plain south-east of the volcano, towards which the space shuttle was flying, came into sight. James continued to reduce the speed, and the final landing phase began, during which the spacecraft hovered above the surface of Mars vertically and touched down after approximately two minutes. The landing itself passed without incident or turbulence, which was a big relief for both the astronauts and the ground station. On Earth, many people were watching this event on television despite the indifference which had followed the initial interest in this third flight to Mars. When the whirling dust had settled, the landscape offered the astronauts a magnificent view. The landing site looked like a stone desert on Earth strewn with sand and rocks. Olympus Mons rose to the north-west, while the three more distant volcanoes towered above the haze of the plains to the south-east.

With the aid of the positioning system, James determined that they had landed only a few yards away from the planned site. Under a thin layer of sand, the surface was level and rocky, which the measurement results of satellites had already indicated before. The space shuttle therefore rested on solid ground, which was critical for a longer stay. The data transmitted to Earth corresponded exactly to what scientists and engineers had expected so that the crew would soon be able to begin its work. Before, however, the astronauts needed sleep and a longer rest in order to gain new strength. During this phase, one crew member remained in the cockpit, while the other two slept. It was Catherine´s turn first to control all necessary functions and to manage the communication with Earth, which was exclusively limited to e-mails due to the long delay in transmission. She also used the time to send messages to her family, for which she had had only little time before landing. Like the other two astronauts, she felt a loss because telephone conversations had become impossible long ago due to the immense distance, but her ability to feel close to others while daydreaming helped her to cope better with the feeling of loneliness. During these hours, Catherine nonetheless became fully aware that more than one year on Mars and the five-month return flight still lay ahead of her. This long time in a fascinating, though desolate and inexorable environment appeared unfathomable and almost threatening to her at the moment. She was glad when her break began and immediately fell into a deep sleep. In her dreams, she not only experienced the landing again, but also moments of her youth in South Carolina and her time in Germany. When she awoke, the tension had subsided, and she felt a sense of trust and confidence in facing what was going to come.

The next day, the astronauts began preparing for a longer stay on Mars. Before they were able to begin exploring the planet, they had to bring in the supplies which had been transported to Mars by unmanned spaceships. According to the ground station, the two supply ships with food and fuel had landed at a respective distance of approximately 3 and 6 miles from the space shuttle. The large Mars vehicle had been converted such that it was able to carry several hundred pounds. Nevertheless, about 10 trips to the two space ships would be necessary to transport all supplies back to the shuttle. It was planned that two crew members would seek out the supply ships, while one remained in the space shuttle.

James and Catherine began to search for the supply ship which had landed farther away. It was the first time that Catherine had seen the Martian landscape outside the space shuttle, and she was just as deeply impressed as during the first hours after landing. They had set out shortly before dawn. For the first time, they saw the sun rise above the horizon and suffuse the atmosphere with reddish, glowing light, which illuminated the dim shapes of hills and rock formations. At a greater distance, the towering silhouette of Olympus Mons rose, whose upper part was already shining in the sunlight and thus formed an even sharper contrast to the deep darkness at the foot of the mountain. Since the supply ship had landed in a higher part of the plain, they drove towards the sunlight, which was slowly descending from the summits of the mountains and hills into the plains and valleys. When they passed the border between shadow and light, the color of the soil also changed from an ashen gray to a pale and finally more brilliant red. After they had reached the supply ship, both astronauts looked over the plains in front of them where the space shuttle had landed. While Catherine was drawn to the alien environment and almost had the impression that she was part of this world, the Martian landscape reminded James of his nightmares of war and destruction, which he had had again after they had landed on Mars. He was glad when he was able to focus on loading the Martian vehicle with the content of the supply ship. Catherine helped him and steered the small forklift which had been delivered to Mars with the supply spaceship. After approximately three quarters of an hour, the vehicle was fully loaded, and they headed back to unload it. The second time, Catherine left for the supply ship together with David.

Meanwhile, it was late in the morning, and the sun had almost reached its zenith. This time span was familiar to the astronauts because a Martian day was about as long as a day on Earth. The sky was a colorful mix of different shades of red and yellow, which was typical at noontime, while the rocks exhibited their full red color. When they got off the Martian vehicle, Catherine said to David:

"I think it's a miracle that we are here on another planet. This is something I would never have imagined 20 years ago."

"I wouldn't have either. Sometimes life leads us down unknown paths and we only understand things when we look back," answered David, and together they looked over the wide plains covered with rocks and boulders.

It took several days until the supply ships had been unloaded and the devices had been set up and connected which allowed them to gain water from the Martian soil. Afterwards, their extensive exploration of the environment was scheduled to begin. It was planned that Catherine and David would first study a hilly region approximately 13 miles to the north of the landing site. Since the two Martian vehicles were too small for the astronauts to spend the night in them, the two would return to the space shuttle at the end of each day. Their tasks during the expeditions, which were set to last about one week and on which they would sometimes be together and sometimes alone, included the extraction and examination of soil samples as well as the precise survey and mapping of the terrain. When they left early in the morning of the first day, the weather and visibility were as good as they had been since their landing so that they soon saw the hill range from afar in the light of the rising sun. After their arrival, they began to take samples and to survey the environment. They made good progress in their work and were therefore able to head back early in the afternoon. Since they had to map another part of the hilly region farther to the north, they chose a different route, which led them through a large sand field with drifting dunes. When they reached the sand field, they noticed that the vehicle handled differently than on the rather rocky ground on which they had traveled so far. Again and again, the wheels sank into the soft sand, and a rising wind blew more sand towards them and began to obscure their vision. The vehicle kept losing speed on the soft ground until it finally stopped. Catherine and David got out and tried to shovel the wheels free, but the wind blew more and more sand in their direction and rendered their efforts hopeless. Fortunately, the gusts were not too strong and did not develop into a sand storm, which would have buried the vehicle. They decided to tell James about the difficulties and wait until the wind died down, which, they hoped, would not take too long. Even though they had both been aware before that such adverse weather conditions could occur, it was different to experience them in reality, and they felt their vulnerability in this alien world. Catherine was glad to know that David was by her side, and David also sensed that Catherine's presence enabled him to cope better with his anxiety. After about half an hour, the wind abated, and both astronauts were able to free the vehicle from the sand and to return to the space shuttle.

After their arrival, they began to examine the soil samples for chemical elements. Scientists hoped that they might reveal traces of life on Mars as well as other relevant information. However, the chemical analysis again delivered disappointing results in that it did not show any indications that life may have existed in this region in the past. Feeling somewhat more confident that they might be able to make a contribution towards understanding the climatic conditions on Mars, they transmitted the weather data recorded by the Martian vehicle to the on-board computer in order to gain insights into the origin of sand storms. After they had finished, all astronauts went to their cabins to rest. According to their schedule, Catherine would map another part of the hill range alone, while James would head on his first expedition towards the system of rift valleys to the south.

In the morning, they both set out for their different destinations. Due to the difficult terrain conditions, James was assigned the large Martian vehicle, while Catherine covered the shorter distance to the hills in the smaller of the two vehicles. Given the difficulties that had been experienced the day before, they had decided that Catherine would choose the shortest and safest way to the hill range, especially since she would be alone that day. After her adventure on the previous day, she could not help feeling slightly anxious and queasy when she began her ride. However, the weather was good, and no signs of an impending change were visible when she arrived at her goal roughly an hour later. As she scanned the large plain, she caught sight of the place where she had almost been surprised by a sand storm the day before. Although she felt an initial sense of insecurity, this feeling eventually gave way to growing relief as the wind became weaker and weaker and finally calmed entirely. As she returned to the space shuttle, dusk covered the surface of Mars with blood-red light before the red sky finally faded into darkness and the stars became visible. At this moment, Catherine felt a deep sense of tranquillity and attachment to the world and those who were close to her. When she reached the space shuttle, all her fear and anxiety had disappeared.

Meanwhile, James had not yet returned from his first excursion to the system of rift valleys, which was about 18 miles away. This was not only the result of the greater distance, but also of the more demanding terrain conditions. The ground here was soft and sandy, which made the ride slower and more difficult. When he arrived at his goal after about two and a half hours, he saw that the slopes of the valleys were steeper than the astronauts and the ground station had assumed before. In some places, pointed rocks protruded from the sand, but most of the slopes were covered by a sand layer which was several yards thick and whose surface looked like the rippled water of a shoaly lake, an appearance caused by the continuous, gently-blowing wind. Today, however, the weather was extraordinarily calm in this region and made the landscape appear treacherously quiet. James began to map the rift valley system and therefore drove a longer distance alongside the valley, which was more than 1,500 feet deep in one spot. There, it narrowed and its slopes gradually became steeper until finally they formed a virtually vertical face, which was approximately 300 feet tall. As James stood there looking down into the ravine, he felt dizzy for a brief moment, a feeling which he knew from his nightmares in which he and the world around him seemed to be engulfed by an abyss. However, this sensation disappeared after a few seconds, and he continued to map the terrain, which he was able to survey particularly well from this point as the edges of the valley rose slightly above the surrounding area. After several hours, he began to make his way back to the space shuttle, reaching it only long after darkness had fallen.

The next day was a quiet day for the astronauts, but they nonetheless used the time to prepare the following expeditions. During her next excursion, Catherine had the task of exploring the plains to the north of the hill range, while James would continue mapping the rift valleys, a project which would take quite a bit of time. Both astronauts were scheduled to leave the next day, while David would remain in the space shuttle.

The weather forecast was good, but such predictions were not at all reliable on Mars because sand storms covering a region of several hundred square miles could occur unexpectedly at almost any time.

When Catherine and James headed in different directions on the following day, visibility was good. However, a slight breeze was blowing and began to whirl up grains of sand in some places. Catherine recalled what had happened several days ago and could not help feeling uneasy. However, there was nothing which would really have indicated a weather change. Therefore, she kept her misgivings to herself, not sure anymore whether her imagination was getting the better of her or not. This time, she would drive farther away from the space shuttle and would need approximately two hours to reach her destination. The two astronauts had therefore left as early as possible so that they would be back not long after nightfall. Catherine's ride proceeded as planned at the beginning. She crossed the hill range about one hour after sunrise and viewed the plains ahead of her above which Olympus Mons rose in the distance. After another hour, she finally arrived at her destination, a point in the middle of a lowland north of the hill range. Sometime after she had begun her work, she became faintly aware of a reddish gleam on the horizon, which was spreading slowly. She did not attach any importance to this phenomenon and attributed it to light changes in the atmosphere, which occurred frequently shortly after sunrise. When she looked up sometime later, however, she noticed that the gleam had become stronger and had developed into a reddish glow, which was illuminating the northern sky more intensively, suffusing the area around the volcano with a dazzling light. She decided to tell David about it, who had also observed the phenomenon from the space shuttle.

"I think this may be the beginning of a sand storm. What would you do if you were in my place?"

"You should return to be on the safe side," he answered.

"Yes. It´s probably for the best. However, I´ll need some time and hope that I´ll reach the space shuttle before the storm becomes worse."

After this short conversation, Catherine returned to her vehicle, hastily loaded her instruments, and left while the reddish glow was intensifying, forming a dense, dark cloud which was moving towards her. At the same time, the wind was blowing stronger and began to whirl up the sand.

James had also noticed the reddish gleam shortly after his arrival. At first, he had not taken it very seriously and had continued his ride along the valley in order to survey the environment from the highest point. Very quickly, however, the red glow in the atmosphere had developed into a reddish-black fog which, coming from Olympus Mons, threatened to engulf the valley and its environment. If James had not known that Olympus Mons had been extinct for eons, he would have taken the beginning of a sand storm for a volcano eruption. Far sooner than he would have expected, the first strong gusts of the storm reached him and began to obscure his vision. He quickly lost all hope of returning to the space shuttle especially since he was at the highest point above the rift valley system and a loss of orientation would have deadly consequences. When he tried to inform David, he noted with dismay that the radio connection had been severed due to the storm which continued to grow more violent by the minute.

Meanwhile, the storm had also reached Catherine, but the wind was not as strong as in the part of the Tharsis region where James was and although visibility was poor, it was still sufficient. In addition, the ground was somewhat rocky and covered by only little sand so that her vehicle hardly sank into the ground. Most importantly, she managed to maintain the radio connection to the space shuttle except for an occasional interruption. David was always informed of her current position, which gave her a certain feeling of security despite her anxiety. Struggling against the wind and the incessant stream of sand grains, she saw bits of her past flash by in her mind, dreams which emerged from the depths of her subconscious and disappeared again, memories of Roger as well as her first experience with a sand storm several days ago. Despite the menacing circumstances, these images offered her solace and gave her the impression that she was part of a stream which had an origin and a destination. She focused on trying to keep the course towards the space shuttle, relying on both her eyes and her navigation system and unconsciously let her thoughts flow freely. Before she realized it, she had already reached the hill range and covered more than half of the way back. Beyond the hills, the storm had calmed such that it took her just another hour to return to the space shuttle where David was anxiously awaiting her.

James, however, was caught in the storm. Over and over again, he tried to free the vehicle from the sand, which was piling up in huge drifts, but the hurricane was too strong and thwarted all his efforts. While he was standing next to the vehicle, he repeatedly heard a strange noise, a loud roaring which reminded him of the noise of fighter jets. He believed this was the constant rushing of the storm, but then he heard the noise of attacking airplanes and moving tanks. "It's only a hallucination," he told himself, but the images began to hypnotize him and the boundaries between dream and reality gradually disappeared. He was still vaguely aware that he was somewhere near the edge of the rift valley, but his sense of danger was waning and nightmares were flooding his mind. The noise began to overpower him, and he saw the threatening shapes of approaching enemy soldiers and tanks in the middle of the sand storm. He moved farther away from his vehicle, which had meanwhile sunk deeply into the sand. The impending threat horrified him, and his only goal was to escape this world at any cost. In the end, he felt himself falling and was no longer able to distinguish whether this fall was dream or reality. Darkness finally enveloped him. When he awoke, it was the middle of the night and he did not know whether hours or days had passed.

From the shuttle Catherine and David were desperately trying to contact him and to determine the precise position of his vehicle. This proved impossible due to the continuing sand storm. It took several hours before the wind calmed down and they were able to locate where James´ vehicle was. In the meantime, James had regained consciousness and was able to communicate with the other two astronauts. He was panic-stricken when he noticed that he was buried up to his chest in the sand and could no longer move his legs. This was shocking news for David and Catherine because they knew that this most likely meant that their stay on Mars would come to an abrupt halt.

At the break of dawn, David and Catherine set out to look for James. The wind had died down, but the drifts formed by the sand storm had become towering, virtually insurmountable obstacles many feet in height, which almost made them lose hope that they would reach their goal. When they finally arrived at the edge of the valley having driven several hours, they saw James´ vehicle, which was almost entirely covered by sand. James had been surprised by a sand avalanche on the steep slope approximately one hundred yards away and had been thrown against a rock. David and Catherine moved slowly on the loose sand repeatedly sinking into the ground up to their knees. They feared triggering a new avalanche and being swept away by the shifting sand. When they reached James, they saw that his space suit and his helmet had been damaged by the fall, but that they were still tight, a miracle which had saved James´ life.

The two of them slowly freed their colleague from the sand and tried to calm him with soothing words and gestures. Since the sand kept shifting, it took a long time until they had freed his legs to a point where they could try to lift him. While doing so, they noticed that he really was paralyzed from the waistline downwards and that he was unable to walk on his own. His spine had obviously been injured during the fall when he hit the rock. David and Catherine decided to use a stretcher to carry him to the vehicle, which proved to be very difficult and dangerous in the deep sand. When they finally reached the Martian vehicle and bedded James carefully on the bottom of the cargo hold, it was late in the afternoon, and the sun was already approaching the horizon. David slowly steered the vehicle through the fine-grained sand, which resembled a liquid mass that threatened to devour everything. Darkness soon fell on the planet, and only the stars and the Milky Way cast their distant, weak light onto the mountains, hills and valleys of the Martian landscape. Despite the distressing situation, the view overwhelmed Catherine with its beauty and instilled a feeling of almost supernatural calmness in her helping her forget their frightening reality for a while. Like David, however, she was relieved when they arrived at the space shuttle and were able to take James to his cabin, where they first placed him on his bed and examined his body for injuries. Except for contusions and a few bruises, he showed no external signs of harm, but the injury to the spinal column, which he had obviously sustained, had most likely caused lasting paralysis, especially since they did not have any possibility of treatment on board the space ship. In addition, the emotional trauma of his ordeal rendered him speechless so that he could not tell Catherine and David exactly what had happened in detail.

After they had taken care of James, Catherine and David informed the ground station of the incident. Everyone there was extremely apprehensive because the astronauts had been away for too long now and had not contacted anyone on Earth. Having sent the message, Catherine and David reflected on the events of the past hours. It was clear to both of them that they would most likely have to end their stay on Mars and return home. Attempting the flight back so long before the scheduled date meant that they would face incalculable risks and dangers as they would be forced to take a different route which would lead them past Venus and possibly expose them to strong solar radiation. At the moment, they could not do much more than wait because it would take some time until the responsible officials and scientists on Earth had developed a plan for their return. The first answer from the ground station arrived after approximately four hours and confirmed what Catherine and David had already suspected: They had to return to Earth as quickly as possible because any further scientific research would be impossible in light of James' severe injury. All necessary preparations were to be made as quickly as possible.

In the coming days, David and Catherine brought all instruments installed outside back into the space shuttle, secured the data of the experiments, and prepared the shuttle itself for the flight back. At the same time, the ground station calculated the route for the voyage to Earth, which would make a Venus fly-by maneuver necessary due to the position of the planets. In addition, they needed to take care of James, who was still unable to move his legs. However, his ability to communicate had improved dramatically and he had been able to describe his accident in detail during a lengthy conversation. The hallucinations before the fall he mentioned only in allusions, but Catherine interpreted his words correctly and presumed that his past trauma had largely contributed to the accident even though it was too painful for him to admit directly. As best she could, she tried to comfort him and to give him hope for the future. It was nonetheless clear to everyone that the flight back would be dangerous and that they would be alone in the vastness of space during which time any mistake could have fatal consequences. Since James could not carry out his duties as a pilot, David and Catherine would have to take over his responsibilities. Even though Catherine was not a trained pilot, she was familiar with the control of the space shuttle, which would allow her to relieve David during almost all phases of the flight.

It took several days until all the preparations were completed and the space shuttle was ready for the return flight. When David and Catherine took their places in the cockpit, it was late in the afternoon and the space shuttle finally lifted off towards the orbit with James strapped onto the bed in his cabin. During the flight through the atmosphere, Catherine's eyes wandered across the volcanoes and valleys of the mysterious planet for the last time. She recalled all the dreams, thoughts, and images connected to them, the sand storms and dangers as well as the memory of landscapes which appeared inhospitable at first glance, but which were of an almost divine beauty and had given her the feeling of being part of a large cosmos more than ever before.

"Nobody would have believed that we would leave Mars so soon," said David.

"No, but nevertheless I don't regret making the journey to come here even though the most difficult part still lies ahead of us," answered Catherine.

«I feel the same. The view is so unique that I would go on this flight again for that reason alone," said David and briefly smiled at Catherine.

After several minutes, they had reached the orbit and prepared for the linkup with the third propulsion stage, which was still orbiting Mars and which they needed for the return to Earth. While the space shuttle was approaching the rocket stage, Catherine reduced the speed. Supported by David, she then connected the propulsion stage to the space shuttle. Both astronauts were glad that this first important maneuver had been accomplished and that the journey to Earth could begin.

While the space shuttle was orbiting Mars, Catherine and David thought of the flight back and their families at home, with whom they had exchanged messages only rarely in the past days and weeks. Catherine's parents and her sister as well as David's family were deeply concerned when they learned what had happened on Mars, and the public also showed great support for the crew again. Catherine tried to calm her family because she knew that newspapers and TV stations were reporting in detail on the dangers of a return at the current moment. Concern was also growing because it had been made public that recent observations had shown a certain increase in solar activity and that the flight path would first lead towards Venus, considerably closer to the sun than previously planned. According to the ground station, however, the risk of a strong solar eruption was low, and the crew hoped that this was true because all three of them knew what damage such an event could cause. An additional worry was the small, though always present danger of a collision with a meteoroid, which was more prevalent during the early phases of the flight. Such an impact could possibly destroy the outer layer of the space shuttle and cause the spaceship to disintegrate during the flight through the Earth's atmosphere.

After several hours, the space shuttle left the Mars orbit, and the long, uncertain return towards Earth began. When Catherine felt the acceleration, she cast a last, short, almost wistful look out of the side window back at Mars, at its deserts which were shining red in the sunlight, and at the volcanoes of the

Tharsis region, from where they had departed a short time ago. While this world, which was no longer quite so unfamiliar to them, receded in the distance, they were again enveloped by the darkness of space with all its faraway and unreachable stars and galaxies.

As planned, Catherine and David took turns controlling the space shuttle. Since the shuttle kept the set course automatically, both had enough time to rest and also to look after James. His ordeal on Mars and the expectation that he would remain paralyzed for the rest of his life made him feel more and more depressed. Even sleep offered no reprieve. Nightmares continued to torment him and when he was awake his conscience plagued him because he feared that his unsolved mental conflicts had endangered the other two astronauts. David and Catherine tried to calm him and assured him that he was not to blame for what had happened and that such strokes of fate could hit anyone. They also let him participate in their work and quite frequently asked him for his advice. Occasionally, this distracted him from his melancholic thoughts.

Meanwhile, several days had passed since their departure. The third propulsion stage, which had generated the necessary acceleration for the flight to Earth, had been discarded, and the space shuttle had already moved far away from Mars, which now looked like a disc whose size was diminishing every day. In this region between the orbits of Mars and Earth, the danger of a collision with a meteoroid was the greatest. Even though the outer layer of the space shuttle was made of specially hardened materials which resisted light impact, a larger meteoroid could wreak havoc. During the two previous missions, the space shuttles had only been hit by particles that were not much bigger than sand grains and had not caused any serious damage. Again on this flight, the astronauts hoped that everything would go well.

As during the flight to the Red Planet, David and Catherine spent some of their free time in their cabins. Despite all the stress they were under, they still even found time to read and to talk to each other. On one of these days, Catherine had listened to music in her cabin for a while before returning to David in the cockpit where she would take over the control of the shuttle in about half an hour. She had just sat down in the copilot's seat when they suddenly felt a strong jolt as if something had exploded in the space shuttle. After a brief moment of confusion, they knew that they had been hit.

Although they remained outwardly calm, they were not able to suppress the fear they felt entirely.

"I think it was a meteoroid," said Catherine.

"It's the most likely explanation," answered David, and James, whom they asked for advice, also believed that this was probably the cause of the jolt. Catherine and David searched the interior of the space shuttle for damage, but they could not find anything. Afterwards, David inspected the outer wall with the aid of the cameras installed there. He quickly discovered the area of the impact and called Catherine so that they could survey the damage together. There was a cavity which looked like a crater, but they were unable to determine how severe the problem was.

"With the camera we can't see how deep the hole is," said David. "And the worst of it is that we don't know if the thermal insulation is still intact and if it will be able to withstand the flight through the Earth's atmosphere."

"This is true, but it also gives us hope that all might still end well," answered Catherine. At the moment, hope was all they had. They knew that it was impossible to repair the damage and that destruction to the insulation could mean death.

Catherine immediately informed the ground station, where the message caused great concern. The engineers on Earth asked the two astronauts to inspect the outside of the space shuttle again with the aid of the cameras, to examine the damage thoroughly and to send pictures to Earth. However, even these images could not provide any conclusive results.

The only thing the astronauts could do was wait and hope. Even though Catherine and David sometimes experienced moments of despair, they were able to overcome them and did not lose their faith in a safe return. When she felt close to hopelessness, Catherine found solace looking at the starry sky, which gave her a feeling of security. At such times, she felt close to her family and to all the people who had been important to her in life, and it helped her that she had learned to take these feelings seriously.

"Do you really believe that we´ll make it back to Earth?," David asked her once.

"I don´t know for sure, but I feel it quite strongly. Something inside of me tells me that we´ll make it."

"I´m also firmly convinced of it," answered David and gave Catherine a brief hug. Before David´s break began, they went to see James, whose emotional state had deteriorated further after the collision and who was still blaming himself for their critical situation. Even if they were not able to free him from his gloomy thoughts, their confidence nevertheless gave him a ray of hope which saved him from falling deeper into despair.

Catherine and David often received messages from their families describing the concerns on Earth. They were told that there were constant reports on the shuttle crew and its fate and that not only relatives, but also people worldwide admired the crew´s stoicism.

During the following weeks, the spaceship continued its flight, crossed the Earth´s orbit and headed for Venus, which the shuttle had to circle first in order to reach Earth after the gravitational field of the planet had changed its course. Catherine and David remained composed and their hope and confidence grew that they would survive, although they did avoid thinking about the minutes when the shuttle would enter the atmosphere. James' condition did not deteriorate any further, and on some days he was even able to get up with David's and Catherine's help and to send some long-awaited mails to his family and friends.

Since their departure from Mars, the sun had grown from a small disc into a fireball, which meanwhile appeared far larger in the sky than the full moon on Earth. At the same time, Venus with its white, shining atmosphere became more clearly visible, while Earth was discernible only as a small, faraway planet. While the "Constellation" was approaching Venus, observations and measurement results on Earth showed initial indications of a possible solar eruption in the near future. Even though this information was still very imprecise and not yet a cause of serious concern, the ground station nonetheless decided to prepare the astronauts for such a danger. In the event of a strong eruption, the crew could withdraw into the team room, which was situated in the center of the space shuttle and had reinforced walls that absorbed the radiation better. The data on the computers had to be secured beforehand, and the computers which were not needed had to be shut down in order to avoid failures and damage. Despite all precautionary measures, the danger of a power outage and thus also of a breakdown of all important control units still existed.

For the time being, however, there was no imminent danger, and the astronauts were able to observe Venus while flying by the planet, whose gravitational field altered the course of the space shuttle such that it headed towards Earth. Catherine and David were sitting in the cockpit as they circled half of the planet at a distance of several thousand miles. They both gazed at the impenetrable layer of clouds shining in the sunlight, which covered a hell that would forever remain inaccessible to humans. They were familiar with the images of the surface taken by unmanned space probes, a surface at the bottom of an ocean of gas which only little light touched even during the day and where temperatures prevailed which would make metal melt. They were greatly impressed by the view of the planet, but it also reminded them of their vulnerability and the hostility of space towards life.

Several days after they had flown by Venus, the astronauts received more disturbing news from Earth, where observatories and satellites had registered growing solar activity. The latest measurements showed more distinctly that a strong eruption was imminent and that it would hit the space shuttle in a dangerous phase of its flight. The ground station ordered the crew to prepare for the event and to protect all important systems of the shuttle as best they could.

At the same time, concerns about the crew members were growing on Earth. At the ground station, a large staff of engineers and scientists continuously discussed the measures to be taken, and the media also reported the latest news almost every hour. Catherine, David and James had difficulties calming their families and friends, especially since their mails inevitably reflected the growing tension on board. In the coming hours, they had just enough time to secure the data on the on-board computers and to shut down all the systems which were not needed before the solar eruption suddenly began. They received the warning from the ground station just in time and immediately sought refuge in the protected team room. Several minutes later, all the lights went out. There was a complete power outage, and the only light they had fell scantily through a small skylight into the team room. It was weak, but it did provide the astronauts with some orientation. Since the room served as a shelter in the event of an emergency, there were three beds attached to the walls which could be folded down.

This would be home to the three astronauts during the days to come.

As a result of the power outage, temperatures in the space shuttle began to sink slowly, but continuously despite the particularly good insulation in the team room. What was most depressing for the astronauts, however, was that all connections to Earth had been severed and no one knew precisely what effect this event would have on the sensitive computers and control units on board the space shuttle and whether a return to Earth would even be possible in case of lasting, severe damage. The astronauts tried to stay calm even in the face of this critical situation and discussed all the options they had and what they had to do after the end of the solar eruption. The longer the eruption lasted, however, the more silent and withdrawn they became. All three often remained lost in thought for a long time. James was tortured by depression and feelings of guilt, and deep down he sometimes even longed to die. David and Catherine, confronted with their own mortality, also began to call their past lives into question. It was the first time that they doubted their decision to become astronauts. However, they also remembered their childhood, the people who were close to them and, despite all doubts, their never dying conviction that there was a thread in their lives which connected all important events and made things whole. After a long period of silence, Catherine said to David:

"Lately, I´ve started to doubt whether my decision to become an astronaut was right. Even though I knew about the dangers, I tried to ignore them, and maybe I was too convinced that we would be able to keep everything under control ourselves."

"I think you made the right decision," said David and expressed what Catherine thought deep down. "We bear the same risk the first flight pioneers did a long time ago. People smiled at them too and thought they were crazy daredevils because they seemed to ignore dangers, but what they did made sense, which nobody would doubt today. Space travel will be regarded in the same way in the future."

"I guess you're right," answered Catherine. "What we do has a purpose which will be seen long after we're gone."

Meanwhile, it had become even colder in the space shuttle, and the temperature began to approach the freezing point. All three of them tried using blankets to keep themselves as warm as possible and hardly spoke to each other. Nonetheless, Catherine and David felt very close to each other, which kept them from falling into the depth of despair even when the cold turned bitter in the following hours and the hope of a safe return to Earth began to dwindle. They spent what seemed like an eternity in their beds until suddenly the lights went on in the team room. The solar eruption was slowly becoming weaker and the electricity supply in the space shuttle had been reestablished. There would still be some occasional short power outages during the hours to come, but little by little the temperatures increased above zero again, and the astronauts began to feel new hope. They still had enough time until landing to reactivate the control systems needed for their return. However, it was questionable whether the on-board computers had survived without damage and whether it was possible to repair their functions such that they would be able to fulfill their tasks. In addition, the radio connection was dead and no one on Earth knew what was happening on board the space shuttle. The astronauts were left entirely to their own devices.

David and Catherine started the computers as soon as they were able to and their fears were confirmed. The solar eruption had wrought havoc and important parts of the control systems no longer worked. The two of them had to try to repair the damaged files and functions the best they could. Their time was limited because the computers and control systems were needed in order to reduce the shuttle speed and to return to Earth. David and Catherine worked feverishly in order to cope with the immense workload and the task of repairing or replacing thousands of files and programs. They both spent hours trying to cope with the problems, but they were making only very little progress and they sometimes asked themselves whether it was not just a fruitless effort because they knew they would probably be unable to solve some problems without the help of the ground station. The radio connection to Earth was still dead, and it was not clear whether it could be reestablished in the near future because the effects of the eruption had also been very strong on Earth. Nonetheless, they did not lose hope and overcame one difficulty after another until they finally reached a point where they could not find a solution for a damaged file which was needed to control the propulsion nozzles. After hours of futile attempts and two virtually sleepless nights, David and Catherine felt a growing sense of desperation given the almost unsolvable problems.

"Sometimes, I´d just like to quit and let what´s going to happen, happen even if it means the end," said David.

"Believe me, I also know the feeling," replied Catherine. "But we can´t give up yet. We owe it to our families and the people on Earth. If we die, death might not be so terrible, but if we´re successful, we still have a large part of our lives ahead of us. We should try to get some rest first and then continue our work starting at a different angle. Maybe we´ll have an idea after we recover."

That decided, they first went into the team room and took care of James, who was still extremely depressed and needed help caring for himself because of his paralysis. Afterwards, they withdrew into their cabins, which they were now able to use again after the radiation levels had dropped, and fell asleep immediately. The next morning, they did indeed come closer to a solution even though progress was slow and they were unable to establish a connection to Earth. It seemed like nothing short of a miracle when Catherine and David finally succeeded in repairing the most important file. They had benefitted tremendously from Catherine's experience as a software developer. Her knowledge in this field had proven invaluable. Both were delirious with joy and hugged each other ecstatically, and even James started to cheer up.

Despite this decisive breakthrough, a lot still needed to be done, and both knew that there would barely be enough time until they reached Earth to prepare the on-board electronics for landing. The situation was compounded by the deep-felt insecurity about whether the space shuttle could land safely following the meteoroid impact or whether it would disintegrate during the flight through the atmosphere. This uncertainty plagued Catherine and David day and night. Sometimes they even dreamed that they were in a spaceship being devoured by flames in its final minutes until they woke up drenched in sweat. As soon as they resumed their work, however, they were distracted to a point where all these fears lost their importance and were replaced by a feeling of emptiness and composure. Once, at the end of a long day together, Catherine said to David:

"Sometimes, I think that it's almost good for us that we're so busy with these computer problems and don't have to constantly think about landing. It means fewer nightmares and almost gives us a sense of calmness and confidence."

"Yes, I've also had fewer nightmares lately," said David and let his gaze wander towards Earth, which was slowly becoming bigger and bigger.

David and Catherine had still had no luck when attempting to contact the ground station, but they did not give up hope that they would eventually be successful. Two days later, Catherine was sure that she had heard noises at the frequency at which the ground station used to communicate with the crew. At first, she thought it was background noise, but then she clearly heard voices and immediately tried to connect to the engineers at the ground station. After several seconds, one of the technicians on duty eagerly responded that he was relieved to hear from her again after all that time. Catherine, David, James, and those responsible for the mission on the ground felt a huge weight fall from their shoulders. The connection which was essential for landing had been reestablished. In the coming hours, Catherine and David were able to receive and send e-mails again, and they informed the ground station and their families in detail about what had happened since the beginning of the eruption. The connection to Earth also made it considerably easier for them to solve the remaining problems in the electronic systems on board the space shuttle. When they had come close enough to Earth, the data from the space shuttle was automatically transmitted to the ground station. This provided insights into potential problems and would help the engineers on Earth to support the astronauts if difficulties occurred.

As they approached Earth during the coming days, the astronauts´ spirits fluctuated between hope and fear. The latter was aggravated by recurring disruptions in the radio signal. James sometimes still had suicidal thoughts, but in the few hours they could spare, Catherine and David were able to give him at least some hope for life after their return to Earth.

Meanwhile, Earth was so close that the oceans and continents were visible. It gave them the feeling that they were near their home planet, but that it was painfully far away at the same time.

"Do you still remember the image of Earth when we left?," Catherine asked David.

"Yes," he replied. "Today, we´ll see it and ourselves with different eyes."

After several days, they had reached the point where the space shuttle would have to reduce its speed significantly in order to enter an orbit around Earth. However, no one knew yet whether this maneuver, which was the prerequisite for the astronauts´ return, would be successful. Even though the technical data transmitted to Earth did not show any abnormal deviations, neither the engineers on Earth nor the crew could be sure that everything would go well. During the last seconds before the ignition of the engines, David and Catherine looked at each other silently and waited for what was going to happen. Despite their fears, however, everything proceeded as planned, and the space shuttle began to orbit Earth. Afterwards they felt relieved even if they were aware that the prospects for a safe return were still highly uncertain.

24 hours remained until the decisive moment when the shuttle would enter into the Earth´s atmosphere. David and Catherine prepared everything for landing and then went to rest in their cabins for seven hours. While his two colleagues were busy with the preparations, James recalled his past life and the flight to Mars. He remembered his ordeal as a soldier, his nightmares, the events on Mars, and his feelings of guilt. In the end, he was not sure whether or not he wanted to return to Earth and awaited the end of the flight with ambivalence.

After the preparations for landing had been completed, Catherine took control of the space shuttle while David´s break began. However, he found as little sleep as James. His thoughts incessantly revolved around landing and his fear of death, but he found some solace in the memories of his sister and the idea that Catherine would be with him no matter what happened. After he had slept during just three of his seven rest hours, he nonetheless felt ready for what was going to come when he relieved Catherine.

In her cabin, Catherine watched the Earth rotate beneath her. The view brought back all the memories of her past, from her childhood up to the present flight. She thought of her parents, Roger, death and what might come afterwards, and also of David, to whom she felt closer than ever before during the flight. The sight of Earth tied all her feelings and thoughts tightly together and made her emotions seem stronger than ever. Even though she was frightened when she thought about what was going to come, she also felt the kind of deep serenity she often experienced when she thought of death, and this feeling was stronger than her fear. After several hours, this tranquillity allowed her to sleep peacefully before her break ended and she returned to the cockpit.

After she had sat down next to David in the copilot's seat, they spoke with their parents one last time and assured them that they firmly believed in a safe return. They both knew that it may be the last time that they talk to them. Catherine was so tense that her voice was shaking when she told her father that no matter what happens he should not worry about her. She regained her composure enough to briefly smile at David through tears before ending the conversation. Afterwards they brought James into the cockpit. During landing, he would be strapped into the seat that was Catherine's during the flight to Mars. In the final conversations with the crew, the engineers at the space center wished the astronauts all the best and tried to appear calm despite the mounting tension. As soon as the space shuttle began to enter the atmosphere, contact with the ground station would be interrupted for several minutes. The technicians on Earth would only have the images from the surveillance cameras to observe what was happening.

David sat in the pilot's seat. It was his job to control the space shuttle during its approach to the space center's runway, while Catherine would be in charge of radio communications during the final landing phase. There were only a few minutes left until they entered the Earth's atmosphere. David, Catherine, and James looked at each other without saying a word and briefly shook hands as a sign of hope and farewell. Catherine looked at David for a moment again and squeezed his arm. They hugged each other one last time with an expression of fear and hope. Then David started the engines. The astronauts felt the deceleration and noticed that the bow of the space shuttle tipped downwards. They saw the Pacific move past them and could make out clouds, cyclones, and the American coast at a distance. The first few minutes were calm, but when the space shuttle began penetrating into the denser layers of the atmosphere, the temperature gradually increased from 68 to 86 degrees, and the first weak turbulence became noticeable. When David looked out of the window, he saw a light glow caused by friction with the denser air. The glow was quickly becoming more intense as the temperature continued to climb. Catherine fixed her gaze ahead and saw that they were approaching the American west coast, all the time being shaken by violent turbulence. A moment later, the space shuttle was almost completely engulfed in flames and the warmth in the interior turned into a scorching, tormenting heat, from which there was no escape. Catherine's entire body stiffened and she was drenched in sweat as were David and James. All three of them were overcome by a near physical, creature-like fear of death. Catherine felt the need to escape impending destruction at all costs, but all she could do was close her eyes in order to be alone with her fear and her despair. When she briefly looked up after a while, the temperature had increased to more than 195 degrees, and it was just a guess that they had flown over the west coast of the United States. Soon afterwards, the temperature began to sink gradually, but they all knew that it was still too soon to breathe a sigh of relief. They could only pray that it would be over soon. But seconds later, the inferno surrounding the space shuttle became fiercer, and the temperature began rising quickly. It was unstoppable. David and Catherine noticed that it reached 212 degrees before they temporarily lost consciousness, a state continually interrupted by moments of awareness in which the terrible reality penetrated into their minds with a cruel violence. Catherine was unable to think of anything else but her pain and the hope that it would all end soon. Tears were streaming down her face, which death was taking hold of, when she heard a loud, distorted noise which announced the imminent disintegration of the space shuttle.

On the ground, all those who were following the flight were meanwhile holding their breath, and everyone expected that it would all be over within a few seconds. The radio connection had been severed some time ago and the images of the space shuttle showed that it was close to disintegration. While the moments were passing like eons, the fireball which hid the space shuttle continued moving towards its goal, which most believed the astronauts would never reach.

When Catherine regained consciousness, she had the feeling that the unbearable burning sensation on her skin had eased off slightly, but she was still too weak to realize this fully. It took more than a minute until she noticed that the temperature had in fact dropped to 160 degrees and was continuing to fall very slowly. The idea that they had survived at first seemed unreal to her, and it took some time until she was completely aware that this new life was no dream, but reality.

The engineers at the ground station had followed the events stunned. They soon noted with astonishment that the space shuttle had not disintegrated and was now decelerating slowly. After the most dangerous phase was over, they frantically attempted to contact the crew, not sure whether the astronauts had survived the extreme conditions on board the "Constellation". Many felt reminded of the time after the solar eruption, but this time the tension was even greater because they all knew that the likelihood that the crew was still alive was small. The minutes passed and their doubts grew until Catherine was finally able to answer them in a feeble voice and assured them that David and James were also still alive. Relief swept over them, but only a few rejoiced as the intense fear and despair had been too severe and had left their traces.

Temperatures in the space shuttle had meanwhile become tolerable, but the astronauts, though fully conscious again, did not say a word. David, Catherine, and James only looked at each other in silence, and their faces showed the toll the encounter with death had taken on them.

For the first time after their endless voyage, they saw terrestrial landscapes with plains, rivers, and mountains. More than ever before, they regarded Earth with all its natural beauty as their home and a place that offered them safety and security after their near fatal ordeal. David controlled the course, but he had little to do. He smiled at Catherine briefly for the first time after they had left the Earth´s orbit. The extraordinarily good weather made the space shuttle glide calmly through the air even though noises during occasional turbulence indicated that the heat while entering the atmosphere had put extreme strain on its structure. After several minutes, they were able to see the coast, and David began to steer the space shuttle towards the runway. The landing itself proceeded without any problems. After their odyssey, the astronauts had returned to the exact spot where they had left Earth many months before. When the space shuttle finally came to a halt, Catherine, David, and James felt profoundly relieved, but also completely exhausted. It took quite some time until the hatch was opened from outside and they were able to leave the space shuttle where they had spent the hardest and most trying days of their lives. For the first time, they felt fresh air again, heard the roaring of the waves and the tweeting of the birds and saw the light of a warm summer day on Earth. It was the beginning of a slow return to a different life.

Soon afterwards, the three were taken to a hospital and examined thoroughly. James was diagnosed with paraplegia. His physicians confirmed that his condition would not improve and that he would never be able to walk again. David and Catherine were exhausted, but physically unharmed and were able to leave the hospital the next day. Upon release, they were happily reunited with their parents and their siblings, who had struggled to keep believing in their safe return and had feared for a long time that they would never see their loved ones again. The time spent with their families afforded them a much needed period of rest and only now, days after landing, were they fully aware of how narrowly they had escaped death. This became even clearer when the space administration began to examine the space shuttle and analyze the flight data. The "Constellation" had been more severely damaged by the meteoroid than had been assumed before and a considerable part of the heat shield had been destroyed in one place. During landing, strain on the fuselage had exceeded the permitted maximum values so far that it was a miracle that the space shuttle had not disintegrated. In addition, it had been mere luck that the weather had been so good on the day of landing because stronger winds or turbulence could have led to a crash. The flight recorder, which also documented important medical data on the astronauts, showed that the temperature in the cabin had increased to almost 265 degrees and that the astronauts had temporarily hovered between life and death.

During the coming days and weeks, David and Catherine recovered well from the physical exhaustion caused by the flight, but emotionally they had both been greatly affected by their experiences. They knew that they shared something which other people, who had not stood on the border between life and death, were unable to understand. More than ever before, they were forced to ask themselves whether they had been at the abyss of death or on the threshold of an afterlife. It was a question they had posed quite a few times before, but which had become far more pressing since the ordeal during the flight. At first, they did not talk about it, but more so than in the past they had the feeling that there was more than just imagination hiding beyond their dreams, even though this seemed difficult to explain at a rational level.

Several weeks later, all three astronauts met for the first time after landing. Apart from his paraplegia, James had also physically recovered, but he was still tormented by feelings of guilt.

"I ask myself every day whether what happened could have been prevented if I had taken my nightmares and my wartime memories more seriously," he told Catherine and David.

"I don't think so," answered Catherine. "Such a flight is extraordinarily stressful for any person, and no one can say beforehand how he will react under these conditions. I think that we all learned that dreams and nightmares are both part of reality and our lives."

These words and the feeling that Catherine and David obviously did not blame him for the events meant a certain comfort for James.

Outside of the space center, a vehement debate about the future of the Mars flights had broken out among scientists, politicians, and the public. Some said that they should be stopped after the flight of the three astronauts had almost ended in a catastrophe. Others, however, believed that such setbacks should not allow anyone to be misled especially since an almost unbelievable series of incidents had occurred during this flight, which was highly unlikely to repeat itself. In addition, the selection process for astronauts was called into question since James' trauma had obviously been overlooked before the flight despite the fact that he had undergone all routine examinations. The psychologists in charge assured the public that they would draw their conclusions and work to improve their methods. At the same time, they also emphasized that it was impossible to see into the depths of the human soul and that science could not offer perfect reliability at this level. In the end, the voices of those who wanted to continue the manned exploration of the Red Planet prevailed. Nonetheless, the decision was made to postpone the flights for a while in order to test technical improvements of the space shuttle, which would protect the astronauts of future missions even better.

After several weeks, David and Catherine resumed their work at the space administration. Clearly they would no longer fly into space. Instead, they would prepare future Mars missions, along with James. Their experiences during the flight had brought them even closer together, and they often met for a long walk at sundown after work. One night, they looked out over the Atlantic and saw Mars, which was just a small dot in the sky over the ocean.

"It's hard to imagine that we were on that planet a few months ago and that people will soon return there," said David.

"Yes, everything seems to be a dream again, but this dream was and is reality. And it has shown us that there are things beyond our world which most of us can't even begin to imagine," replied Catherine.

"You are right, and there are probably only a few people who understand this as well as you do," said David and hugged Catherine.

THE PHANTOM

Completely and utterly exhausted, the young woman walked through the forest, across meadows and through thick undergrowth in the light of the full moon. She was unaware that she had lost her way and did not seem to notice her injuries which had been caused by thorny brushwood. She continued to walk, stumbled, picked herself up, hit a tree, and fell on her back, unconscious. The moonlight illuminated the pale figure while the bitter cold of the February night slowly and mercilessly took possession of her body.

The next morning, forest inspector Joachim Hartmann left for a routine inspection in the Kaiserslautern state forest, which would lead him into a remote area in a section known as "Holy Cross". As soon as he arrived, he began to inspect the trees and returned to his all-terrain vehicle after an hour. He put his maps and lists on the passenger seat and was just about to climb into the driver's seat when he realized that he had actually needed less time than planned. It was the perfect opportunity to check a spruce tree plantation which had been set up two years ago. It was several hundred yards away from the forest road where he had parked his car and could only be reached by trekking along a rugged path. Upon arrival, he noticed a track which looked as though it belonged to a human being. He was taken aback for a moment, but then he convinced himself that it must have been left by a mushroom collector even though he asked himself why anyone would look for mushrooms here.

He continued inspecting the trees and while walking along the plantation he came across the strange footprint again. It was not straight, and it seemed that the person who had walked along here had an insecure gait. Curiosity got the better of him and he decided to follow the footprint, which led him to the body of a young woman about 100 feet away. She looked as if she were between the ages of 17 and 20 years and appeared dead at first glance. She was emaciated, her clothes were torn, and her matted, brown, shoulder-length hair hung deep in her face, which was covered in coagulated blood. She had apparently injured herself severely in the thick, thorny bushes in front of the spruce plantation. She lay on her back next to a half-rotted tree trunk with her arms stretched out. The forest inspector jumped back in horror. Finding a corpse had always been one of his worst nightmares. Still, he mustered all his strength, felt her neck for a pulse and tried to find out whether she was still breathing. She was alive. Her pulse and respiration were still weakly perceptible. He quickly pulled his cell phone out of his pocket and called an ambulance. Then he bent down over the young woman, took his coat off and covered her in order to prevent her body temperature from dropping any further. He asked himself what had happened to her and how she had ended up here. He stayed with her for several minutes before heading back to the forest road so that he could lead the paramedics and the emergency physician to her. Twenty minutes later he was showing the medical assistants and the doctor the way across meadows, brushwood, and thickets. They used a stretcher to carry the unconscious woman through the thick vegetation to the ambulance. There, the physician examined her briefly.

"It was good that you found her," he said to the forester. "She is suffering from hypothermia and wouldn´t have survived much longer in her very weak condition."

Meanwhile, a police car had arrived. The policewoman and her partner regarded the emaciated woman full of compassion and said:

"Thank you for notifying us. Our people from the criminal investigation department will contact you later."

The ambulance rushed the patient to the hospital, where she was treated in an intensive care unit without regaining consciousness. The next day, two detectives visited Joachim Hartmann and briefly interrogated him again about his discovery.

"Do you know who she is and how she got there?," he asked.

"No, we don´t know anything about her yet, and at the moment we have almost no time to investigate a missing person´s case. The so-called phantom is keeping us busy. I´m sure you´ve heard about it."

"Yes, of course... this almost eerie woman who commits one murder and one robbery after the other."

"Right. We would be glad if all our cases were as harmless as this one. Maybe the poor girl was a drug addict or ran away from home and got lost in the forest."

The detectives said goodbye to Joachim Hartmann and returned to their office, which was in a state of frenzy. There had been another burglary in the region where the so-called phantom had been involved. This phantom was on the most-wanted list and was being hunted by a large special task force. This time, not only food and money, but also several weapons had been stolen from a gun club. This worried the detectives because the phantom was considered extremely cruel, dangerous, and violent. Her DNA had been found frequently at the scenes of heinous crimes beginning with the assassination of a retiree who had been attacked and throttled in her house in Ludwigshafen eight months ago. A few weeks later, the trace of the phantom was secured on two corpses found near an interstate highway in the Frankfurt region. In both cases, different accomplices had accompanied the unknown person, but both times the perpetrators had ruthlessly killed their victims using brute force. The extreme violence made the fact that the DNA of the phantom was clearly female even more astonishing. However, this was not the only extraordinary aspect of this case. The same woman had been committing burglaries and robberies with different accomplices all over southern Germany and sometimes even in neighboring Alsace or Lorraine for the past eight months. During the burglary in the gun club, she had been in the company of different criminals again, as DNA tests had proven. Who was this woman, and what did she look like? There were no witnesses who had seen her close up, and none of her accomplices had been captured so far. Several witnesses had stated, however, that they had seen a rather delicate person with short hair, possibly a woman, and with their help a computer image had been created which showed the potential appearance of the phantom. Detailed investigations had led to the result that this composite sketch of the "unknown female person" resembled a 19 year old who had left her parents´ house about 20 months ago and had since disappeared. The young woman, whose name was Daniela Paolini, came from Mannheim. According to the investigations she had disappeared without a trace after severe disputes with her classmates and her mother. She had been described by some of her fellow students as very aggressive and violent. This depiction was confirmed by a group of young people with whom Daniela had lived after her disappearance. She had left the group after fierce disputes approximately eight months ago and had been roaming around alone ever since. It was also known that while she was in school, she had trained in martial arts intensively for several years and had been very successful at jiu-jitsu championships. According to her trainers and clubmates, she had developed extraordinary strength and stamina given her weight and her rather delicate stature. All these were characteristics which fit the phantom exactly, but there was no proof that Daniela Paolini was really the same person. For this reason, she was officially being sought after only as a witness. Despite all their efforts, the detectives on the task force had not been able to secure DNA traces of Daniela. They therefore decided to question parents, friends, and acquaintances again hoping to find suitable traces or at least some indication which could link Daniela to the phantom. In addition, witnesses were being sought via the media who had seen Daniela and could provide information about her. So far, however, the detectives had not received any useful tips and they began to interrogate those who knew Daniela again.

Chief detective Thomas Overmann and his partner, chief detective Judith Breitling, visited Daniela's mother. She swore that she no longer owned any objects where DNA material from Daniela could be found:

"We moved about a year ago. Before the move, we threw out everything that belonged to Daniela."

"But she was your daughter... You must have saved at least something," said Judith Breitling.

"No, nothing except a few photos, which you've already examined. In addition, my relationship with my daughter was and is strained."

"Why?," asked Thomas Overmann.

"She didn't want to have anything to do with my new partner and was far too rebellious."

"What do you mean?"

"Well, she always had her own mind and didn't accept the authority of my partner."

"Were there any concrete reasons for the disputes?"

"No, otherwise we're a happy family. There was no reason for Daniela's aggressive behavior."

"Has Daniela ever become violent?," asked Judith Breitling.

"No. But sometimes she yelled at my boyfriend, and several times he jokingly said that he wouldn´t want to have a serious argument with her because you never knew how she might react…"

Afterwards, the two detectives went to see Daniela´s former boyfriend Benjamin Frankenstetter. He was a high school student from Mannheim, with whom Daniela had had a relationship for a year. They asked him about objects which could possibly contain genetic material, but their hopes were dashed.

"These photos have already been examined by your colleagues. There are no traces left," said Benjamin. The photos taken during a bicycle tour showed Benjamin, a tall, slender young man with dark brown hair and brown eyes, next to Daniela, who was delicate and considerably smaller. At that time, she had short brown hair and her blue eyes gave her the appearance that she was dreaming.

"This is a beautiful photo," said Judith Breitling. "Another question: Has Daniela ever been aggressive or violent towards you?"

"No, never. We actually never had any arguments. She was the sweetest girl I ever met and she was starved for attention. She needed the warmth and closeness she didn´t get at home. If you ask me, there´s no way she could have anything to do with the so-called phantom."

Then, something suddenly came to his mind. "I do have something Daniela came into contact with." He opened his wardrobe closet and showed the detectives a large stuffed mouse with a heart on its chest.

"Cute," said Judith Breitling.

"Yes," answered Benjamin with a sad and at the same time faraway smile. "But unfortunately it probably won´t help you because I had to wash it about seven months ago when I got it dirty while I was renovating my room."

"That's too bad," said Thomas Overmann. "Why did you actually break up, and why did Daniela leave her mother and Mannheim?"

"Oh, that's hard to say... I had the impression that we weren't really a perfect match... and anyway she always had problems with her mother. That's why she finally ran away from home."

"Once you had a dispute with some other teenagers, in which Daniela was also involved. What was the cause of this argument?"

"Well, there had sometimes been problems in school before, and one evening we happened to meet these guys on the banks of the Neckar. I think we all had drunk a bit too much. One of them shoved Daniela a couple of times, and she hit back. Maybe she overreacted a little bit."

"At that time, the story sounded somewhat different..."

"Unfortunately I don't remember all the details. That was too long ago."

After this conversation Thomas Overmann and Judith Breitling interrogated Daniela's trainer. He was also unable to help them in their search for DNA traces, but they used the opportunity to ask him some questions:

"How was Daniela's relationship with her clubmates?"

"Good. I know her as a modest, reserved, and sensitive girl. Since she was very talented and successful, there were of course also envy and feelings of rivalry among the others, but she always tried to avoid arguments."

"Do you believe that she could become violent?," asked Thomas Overmann.

"No. Sometimes, however, it happens that teenagers change significantly. I've also seen such cases."

Afterwards, the two detectives questioned the group of young men who had been involved in the dispute with Daniela and her boyfriend. When the three teenagers were seated in front of them, they began to address their questions to the one who had been considered the leader of the group at that time:

"Mr. Koenig, some time ago you had an argument with Daniela Paolini and her boyfriend Benjamin. Please tell us again what happened."

"Well, we had had a lot of problems with Benjamin in school before. He used to provoke us. On that evening, we met the two on the banks of the Neckar, and they started insulting us. Then Daniela came up to me and told me to leave. She kept coming closer and closer, and I thought that she might use one of her martial arts techniques to throttle me or to knock me down. So I pushed her away, and then she knocked two of my teeth out."

"The police considered this incident as a case of self-defense by Ms. Paolini," said Thomas Overmann.

"They just couldn't imagine that a girl would start a fight with a boy who is 6 feet 8 inches tall and weighs more than 220 pounds. But since Daniela has now shown her true colors, maybe you'll see things somewhat differently."

"But even if one assumes that Daniela could have become violent towards you, the question remains why the two would have started a dispute with a group of three strong men," replied Judith Breitling.

"But it was that way," answered the young man, and the others nodded in agreement.

On the same day, Thomas Overmann and Judith Breitling also interrogated the group of young people with whom Daniela had roamed around for approximately a year. They had also thrown away or destroyed all objects that had belonged to Daniela. The leader of the group described Daniela as aggressive and even ruthless:

"At the beginning, things went pretty well. But then she always started arguments with Tina because she was obviously jealous of her. And finally she beat her up twice so badly that she vomited and fainted afterwards. If we hadn't interfered, she would have killed Tina."

"Those are serious accusations. Are you aware of that?," asked Judith Breitling.

"But they're true," said Tina. "It took me several minutes to wake up, and afterwards I couldn't eat anything for two days." Tobias, the group leader, added:

"She picked a fight with me once too and almost broke my arm."

"What was the reason for this argument?," asked Thomas Overmann.

"She was drunk again, and I asked her to clear her stuff away because there was hardly any space in the tents."

"Why didn't you report these incidents to the police?"

"We deal with our problems without the police. In addition, she left a few days later anyway."

"Why?"

"We told her clearly that she should hit the road, which she eventually did, but not without threatening to get even with us before."

After the young people had left, the two detectives briefly exchanged their opinions.

"I think that a lot doesn't add up here," said Judith Breitling.

"Yes, you're right. Daniela's personality doesn't seem to match the character of the so-called phantom."

"Right. Based on the descriptions of the adults and her boyfriend, I have the impression that she is far too sensitive to commit such crimes. And I believe that the teenagers are hiding something or not telling the truth. A lot of things don't add up in this case."

"Yes. There's a lot that doesn't make sense in this entire phantom story. The unknown woman cooperates with accomplices that are never the same, often commits crimes at places which are far apart and doesn't leave any other traces except her DNA. I think that there are other possible explanations like contamination of the samples, which we haven't followed up on sufficiently so far."

"I agree with you," said Judith Breitling. "Unfortunately, however, we're alone. Our colleagues and the boss especially still firmly believe in the phantom theory."

"It's good that at least we're in agreement," said Thomas Overmann.

"That way I'm not the only one who gets on the others' nerves," replied Judith Breitling, and they both laughed.

At a meeting the next day, Thomas Overmann and Judith Breitling told their 20 colleagues in the task force about their results and their doubts:

"We couldn't find any DNA traces of Daniela, and the statements from her mother, her trainer, her former boyfriend, and the young people she lived with make it appear rather doubtful that she could be implicated in the so-called phantom case. In addition, the allegations of the young people don't seem credible. Moreover, we both still believe that there are too many inconsistencies in the cases in which the unknown woman was allegedly involved and that other explanations, such as contamination by strangers, haven't been sufficiently examined yet." An icy, embarrassed silence followed. Finally, Christian Siebert, the director of the task force, said:

"We carefully secured traces at all crime scenes, and we're continuing to investigate all leads. We've already pursued the idea of potential contamination and had hundreds of cotton swabs tested for remnant DNA. However, these examinations were inconclusive. We have to assume that the DNA found proves the presence of a serial criminal. DNA analysis is still one of the best methods of crime scene investigation, whose results are guaranteed with certainty. As far as the identity of the phantom with Daniela Paolini is concerned, it's still just a theory and that's why she's only being sought after as a witness. Your investigations haven't provided any evidence that proves that she didn't commit the crimes. There are some signs which indicate that she might have had a certain inclination towards violence even before she disappeared."

"We doubt that very much, to put it mildly," said Judith Breitling.

"In any case, objective DNA traces remain which belong to a female person and which are still forcing us to follow this lead in our investigations," replied Christian Siebert. The other members of the task force seemed to agree and the question was settled.

The search for the phantom and Daniela continued and soon took a new turn. Three days later, the DNA of the unidentified person was found in the hut of a fishing club where two members of the club had been attacked and almost killed the night before. The attackers had clearly resorted to brute force because all indications showed that a fierce struggle had taken place between the two members of the club and the offenders. During the days that followed all members of the task force were busy following leads and attempting to establish potential connections to other crimes which the mysterious woman had been involved in. Despite an intensive search, however, no other traces were found which could have been attributed to the phantom. In addition to the "unknown female person", only one other perpetrator had been at the crime scene who had not been implicated in any other crime allegedly committed by the serial criminal. This confirmed the doubts Thomas Overmann and Judith Breitling had, which none of their colleagues seemed to share.

"With every new case, the inconsistencies increase," said Thomas Overmann.

"This is true," answered Judith Breitling. "In particular, the question arises how a woman witnesses have described as being rather delicate can develop the kind of physical strength the offenders displayed during this attack."

"Obviously the opinion seems to prevail that people with a delicate build can sometimes be very strong as well."

"Yes, but if we consider it realistically, it seems rather implausible in this case. I used to do martial arts myself, and I had the experience that young women are sometimes also strong and can beat men in sports. But according to the evidence, the woman who was allegedly involved in this crime would almost have had to be a monster because the two club members were extremely tall, strong, and athletic and defended themselves ferociously. All this makes it far more likely that the attackers were muscular, aggressive male criminals."

"This is certainly true, but unfortunately our opinion is still regarded with little understanding," said Thomas Overmann.

During the coming days, the phantom did not allow the detectives to rest. Only two days after the attack on the members of the fishing club, her DNA was secured in the gymnasium of a high school. There had been a burglary which had caused only little damage. Some teenagers had been arrested after this incident who insisted, however, that no woman had been involved in the burglary and that no girl and no young woman had ever belonged to their group. Thomas Overmann and Judith Breitling now sensed that a few colleagues were beginning to have their doubts, which unfortunately they only expressed in private. During the meetings, the official opinion was still that the unknown person had committed the crimes. Thomas Overmann and Judith Breitling felt the open hostility when they tried for the last time to make themselves heard and to emphasize the numerous inconsistencies, which had grown in number since the last case.

"Do you want us to start from scratch again and forget the investigative work of many months?," asked the director of the task force.

"No, but we have to at least seriously discuss other possibilities," replied Judith Breitling.

"I think you should openly declare that our past efforts have failed," said a colleague, and another one added:

"How can you still seriously doubt objective scientific results? Are you living in the Middle Ages?"

"Well, it´s also the Middle Ages if you believe that a young woman has almost magical strength. The idea existed several hundred years ago. At that time, such women were called witches," said Judith Breitling.

"These are completely absurd and irrational arguments pulled out of thin air. You´re just making fools of yourselves," answered a colleague, and the others nodded.

A few days later, the DNA of the phantom was found on a beer can which had been left in a garden shed near Darmstadt after a burglary and at the door handle of a club gymnasium near Kaiserslautern, whose locker room had been ransacked by burglars. Two hours had passed between the two burglaries, and the second crime had obviously been committed by a group of teenagers. Witnesses claimed to have seen a person among these young people who seemed to fit the description of the series perpetrator. Some detectives considered this a confirmation that the unknown woman had in fact committed the crimes which were ascribed to her even if the traces did show that completely different persons had aided the phantom in the burglaries. This aroused doubts among many colleagues, but still nobody dared to question the phantom theory openly, and Thomas Overmann and Judith Breitling also remained silent after the last discussion so as not to increase the tensions within the group. Only once did Judith Breitling say casually to a group of colleagues:

"If this unknown person doesn't exist, the real criminals are probably laughing their heads off." The looks of some colleagues indicated that they agreed, but nobody answered her.

After only two days the case took a turn which many had feared and some had expected for a long time. The members of the task force were at a meeting when the message arrived that DNA material of the phantom had been secured again after a bank robbery in Wiesbaden and at the site of a daytime burglary near Freiburg more than 150 miles away. These events had both taken place at exactly the same time. At first, they were all dumbfounded when they heard the news, and some were extremely upset because it was undeniable now that months of hard work had been in vain and that the investigations would have to start from the beginning again. After a minute of dead silence, the director of the task force finally said:

"We all know what this news means, and the best we can do is to accept reality. It means that our investigations will have to head in an entirely new direction in the future and that we also have to find out how such a huge number of mistakes could have been made. Last, but not least, we need to know who the wrong DNA traces came from."

Several members of the task force were then commissioned to find the source of potential contamination, while others were ordered to continue investigating the cases of the severe crimes which had wrongly been attributed to the unknown woman. The search for Daniela Paolini was terminated as were any inquiries about a possible connection between her and the phantom.

This sudden twist of events also changed the attitude of the team towards Thomas Overmann and Judith Breitling. Although the two detectives had become outsiders, many of their colleagues now respected and even admired them because they had been the only ones who had expressed what many had thought or at least allegedly always suspected.

The next day, the dissolution of the phantom was also the biggest story in the media. In TV broadcasts and newspapers, the latest development was reported on in detail, and potential reasons for this unprecedented series of mistakes and false conclusions were sought. Three days later, the source of the phantom DNA was found. It was an employee in a company where cotton swabs which were used to collect DNA at crime scenes had been manufactured and packed. At least this part of the case had finally been solved, but otherwise the detectives were still at the beginning of long, difficult investigations.

The young woman who had been found unconscious in the forest several weeks before did not know anything about all these developments. She was no longer in the intensive care unit, and her condition had meanwhile improved considerably, but she had still not regained consciousness. Only two days after it had been made public that the phantom had never existed did she slowly begin to come out of the coma. When she was able to speak again, she asked a nurse where she was and how she had gotten to the hospital.

"You were found unconscious in the forest," answered the nurse. "Do you remember?"

"Yes... very faintly," said the young woman and closed her eyes. A female physician came, examined her briefly and said:

"It's good that you're awake and responsive again. This is a big step forward for you. However, we still have a problem: Despite all our efforts, we still don't know your name, and the police haven't been able to help us either. Could you tell us your name? This would make a lot of things easier for us."

The young woman thought for a moment, struggling to cope with all the thoughts and impressions confronting her. Then she said:

"Yes, of course… my name is Daniela Paolini." The physician looked at her in disbelief, and Daniela became alarmed because she sensed that something obviously was not right even though she had no explanation for the puzzled expression in the eyes of the doctor. The physician noticed her agitation and said:

"Excuse me… I´ll be back in a moment."

In the staff room, she met two nurses and a colleague and said:

"The patient who was in a coma is Daniela Paolini."

At first, the answer was bewildered silence, but then her colleague said:

"Whatever… she can´t be the phantom. By now everyone knows that this mysterious woman never existed. In addition, she´s been in the hospital for several weeks and therefore couldn´t have committed any crimes. The only question is how we´re going to tell her the entire story because she can´t know what happened in the past weeks and why her name was mentioned in the media. In addition, we have to notify the police."

After this conversation, the physician and her colleague went back into Daniela´s room. The female doctor said:

"Excuse me for the temporary confusion. It was caused by events in the past weeks which of course you wouldn´t know about… The problem was that you were being searched for by the police…"

"What?," asked Daniela in dismay.

"Don´t worry. The misunderstanding has meanwhile been cleared up, and it´s obvious that you don´t have anything to do with any crimes. The police were just unable to find an explanation for things after your disappearance."

After Daniela had calmed down, she asked the physician to tell her more about what had happened. When she was finished she said to Daniela:

"You'll certainly understand that we had to inform the police. The detectives will probably ask you some questions."

"Yes, I understand… my God, I didn't know anything," answered Daniela, who gradually began to comprehend what this meant for her.

When the news that Daniela Paolini had been in a hospital for weeks reached the task force, the detectives knew that another part of the puzzle would be solved soon. Thomas Overmann and Judith Breitling were asked to interrogate Daniela because they were most familiar with her life story and the people who knew her. At the hospital, they introduced themselves and told her again what had happened and why they wanted to ask her questions. Daniela was still overwhelmed by what she heard and said:

"If I had known that, I would have returned home or contacted the police."

"Well, meanwhile everything has been clarified, and we know that you can't have anything to do with the so-called phantom. Nevertheless, it would of course be important for us to find out how you ended up in the forest near Kaiserslautern and how this misunderstanding came about," said Thomas Overmann, and Judith Breitling asked Daniela:

"Would you like to tell us your story?"

"Yes, of course… Where should I begin?"

"Right at the beginning, in your childhood," answered Judith Breitling.

"Well, I was born in Mannheim and grew up there with my sister, who is three years younger. My mother's parents came from a place near Rome, but my mother spent most of her youth in Germany. She never got married, but she had several partners over the years. My father was the second one. She left him when I was 13 years old and in 7th grade. A little later, she met her new boyfriend, who moved in with us soon afterwards. The first arguments started right away because he would drink and then start swearing at my mother, my sister, and me. Sometimes, he also tried to beat us. When that happened, my sister and I would lock ourselves in my room until he had calmed down somewhat or fallen asleep. We also had repeated disputes with my mother because she had no understanding for us and often defended her boyfriend even though he sometimes beat her, too."

"Your mother told us later that her relationship with you had been severed and that you had become aggressive towards her partner," said Thomas Overmann.

"As I said, there were sometimes disputes with my mother for the reasons I mentioned, and when her boyfriend swore at me or my sister, I yelled back and tried to protect my sister. At that time, I could hardly stand it at home and frequently went to a sports club where I had been doing jiu-jitsu for about two years. I enjoyed this sport a lot, and it helped me to forget the problems at home for a few hours. Sometimes I trained jiu-jitsu every day, went on long-distance runs and rode my bike. I also had several friends at this club, which was very important for me at that time."

"Your hard training really paid off… You were very successful in sports and won several championships," said Judith Breitling.

"Well…," answered Daniela and blushed slightly. Judith Breitling smiled and said: "Tell us more … Why did you end up running away from home?"

"One reason was that the arguments at home kept getting worse. My mother's boyfriend drank more and more and became totally unpredictable. Sometimes he threw things at us, and on some days the entire apartment stank like alcohol. In addition, there was often nothing to eat because my mother hadn't bought anything or because her partner had invited friends and they'd eaten everything up. Then my sister and

I had to organize something... yes, and then the story with Benjamin began..."

"We'd like to know what exactly happened at that time. Benjamin was very close-lipped and obviously didn't want to tell us much," said Judith Breitling.

"Should I start right at the beginning again?," asked Daniela.

"Yes, please," said Judith Breitling.

"Well... actually everything began three years before I got to know Benjamin. At that time, I had a... somewhat romantic friendship with Andrea, a girl from a parallel class. We liked each other very much and spent a lot of time together. She was the first person except for my sister and my father who really meant something to me. Even though I wasn't used to these romantic feelings, I never believed that I was a lesbian, and Andrea probably didn't think so either. Of course, we never had sex or anything like that...," said Daniela, slightly embarrassed.

"Yes, I understand," answered Judith Breitling. "That's not really uncommon at that age. How did your classmates react?"

"They spread rumors and sometimes also said quite openly that I was probably a lesbian. The rumors continued even after Andrea had moved away from Mannheim and the contact had broken off. Two years after my friendship with Andrea had ended, I got to know Benjamin, a boy from our school who was one year older. He was familiar with these rumors, but he didn't allow himself to be misled by them. Benjamin was all enthusiastic about sports like me and rode his bike for hours every day. We headed out together more and more often and spent almost every weekend going on bike tours in the Palatinate and the Odenwald. During these trips, we got very close to each other, of course...," said Daniela and blushed.

"The first great love...," answered Judith Breitling.

"Yes, but the trouble soon started because Benjamin had

problems with some boys in his class, who were always harassing him. They took things away from him or tried to start fights... And then there was that episode at the Neckar."

"These young men later stated that you and Benjamin had provoked them...," said Thomas Overmann.

"No, that´s not true! We were both afraid of these guys. They were tall and extremely strong, and we knew that we hardly stood a chance against them. They came up to us and began hassling us right away. Two of them got in front of Benjamin and had fun intimidating him. The third one, the gang leader, came walking towards me and said: 'Oh, who is this? Benjamin´s new girlfriend... Come on, Benjamin, show us that you´re a man and protect her if you dare.' Then he shoved me a couple of times... Finally, he grabbed me by my sweatshirt and tried to push me down. He was about 6 feet 8 inches tall, muscular, covered in tatoos, and stank like alcohol. I was terrified... and slammed my fist into his face with all my might. He staggered backwards, stumbled over something on the ground and fell. During this chaos, Benjamin was also able to free himself, and we ran away as fast as possible. The next day, the police came and told me that I had knocked two teeth out of Jason, the gang leader."

"That was self-defense," said Thomas Overmann.

"The police officers told me the same thing, but nevertheless this was only the beginning of the real trouble. I constantly got calls and text messages where I was threatened and called 'lesbian slut', 'dirty bastard', or 'perverted sow'. Rumors started that Benjamin was gay because he was friends with me. This harassment reached its first peak when pictures with nasty comments were spread on the internet which showed me having sex with girls and Benjamin masturbating. At school, other students gave Benjamin the 'desperate warning' to end the relationship with me."

"Didn't anybody do anything about this?," asked Thomas Overmann.

"The principal said that he couldn't do anything because there was no evidence which proved that in fact classmates were responsible for these insults."

Thomas Overmann shook his head and asked Daniela to continue.

"It got worse. One night, Jason's clique must have ambushed Benjamin on a bike path he used every day. In any case, four guys pulled him off his bike and beat him up. They kept beating him and kicking him in his stomach even after he was already lying on the ground. He had several broken ribs and internal injuries and had to spend more than a week in the hospital."

"Benjamin reported the attack to the police at that time," said Thomas Overmann.

"Yes, but there was no proof that it had really been Jason's gang, and the investigation was closed."

"Yes, unfortunately. We know," said Thomas Overmann. "What happened then?"

"Benjamin continued getting threats. He constantly received anonymous text messages and mails where 'bloody retaliation' was announced, and he was told over and over again that this had just been the beginning. One day, he came to me…," said Daniela, fighting back her tears. "He came to me and said: 'I can't stand this any longer. I can't take it anymore. Maybe they'll finally leave me alone if we don't meet anymore.' He asked me whether I would be mad at him if we didn't see each other at least for a while. I was shocked and felt that it was the end of the world for me. But I understood him and didn't want even more to happen to him. We both decided that we would only talk on the phone and maybe see each other secretly once in a while. Right around this time, things at home began getting worse. My mother's partner became violent more often and beat her frequently when he was drunk, which was often. At that time, my sister had her first boyfriend and often slept at his house. In this situation, Benjamin had been my only support, you know?"

"Yes, of course," said Judith Breitling. "This is a really bad story, and it also explains why Benjamin didn´t want to make any statements. When we interrogated him, I had the impression that he had been intimidated... In any case, you ran away from home in complete despair after these events."

"Yes, exactly. I was at the end of my rope and couldn´t stand it anymore in Mannheim, at school, or at home. So I grabbed all my savings, 1,000 euros altogether, and took the train to Saarbrücken. Actually, I only wanted to get away and thought that I might go on to France from there."

"And in Saarbrücken, you met these young people," said Judith Breitling.

"Yes. They talked to me at the station and asked me where I was heading. I liked them, and since I didn´t know where to go, I joined their group. They were slightly older than I was, between 19 and 21, and told me that they lived under bridges or in tents and generally traveled from one town to the next. There were two girls and five boys in the group, who were unemployed or had problems with their families, classmates, or at work and wanted to lead an entirely different life, at least for a while. I slept in a tent with Sabrina, one of the two young women. We made money by making music in the streets or just begging. I also used to play the guitar and sing once in a while, and some people really gave us something..."

Judith Breitling smiled and said: "You traveled through southwestern Germany for almost one year with these young people."

"Yes, a little more than eleven months. We got around quite a bit and even survived the winter pretty well in our tents and sleeping bags. But over time some tensions developed in the group..."

"It seems that you had disputes with another young woman, who later stated that you had beaten her up," said Thomas Overmann.

"What?," asked Daniela in dismay. "I would never have fought with Tina, let alone beaten her up."

"We believe you," said Thomas Overmann. "How did these arguments between you and Tina come about?"

"The reason was Tobias, who was sort of the secret leader of the group. Tina said that I was trying to get involved with him even though this was not true at all. On the contrary, I didn't want to have anything to do with him even though he always made passes at me. I outwardly ignored his advances and hoped that he would eventually stop even though he sometimes kissed me or touched me against my will. This made Tina jealous. She blamed me for my behavior, bad-mouthed me and told the other group members that I was a back-stabbing liar. As a result, some in the group avoided me, but others, like Sabrina, stuck by me. Finally the problems with Tobias became worse. He kept trying to touch me or to hold on to me and sometimes he even sneaked into our tent at night. Once in a while Sabrina and one of his friends would tell him to stop it. Most group members, however, didn't dare to confront him openly. One night he came into our tent while Sabrina wasn't around. He had drunk too much and asked: 'Hey Daniela, how about it?' Then he pulled his pants down and jumped on top of me. I begged him to stop, but he wouldn't listen to me. In the end I did what I had practiced countless times during training. I got a hold of one of his arms and freed myself. Then I jumped up, grabbed my stuff, and ran away. Since we had set up our tents in the forest at that time, I spent the first night on a meadow not too far from our camp. In the morning I went to the nearest town and bought a tent, a camping stove, and some books. Fortunately I still had enough money because I hadn't spent much in the past months. Then I went back to the forest because I just wanted to be alone after all these events. Most of the time I stayed in the region around Kaiserslautern, which I knew quite well from my bike tours with Benjamin. There was a little town where I frequently bought food at a small convenience store. The owner obviously liked me. Once she asked me where I lived and what I did. I told her that I lived in a tent in the forest because I couldn´t stand it any longer at home or in school. She seemed to understand that and often gave me some free food and drinks."

"Did you never feel lonely in the forest?," asked Judith Breitling.

"Sometimes, and I missed Benjamin a lot, of course. But I knew that a relationship with him was impossible at the moment given all the problems and circumstances, and I needed time to gain some distance after all that had happened in the past months. In addition, I didn´t want Benjamin to encounter any more difficulties or find himself in danger. That´s why I didn´t contact him anymore after I left Mannheim even though it was really hard for me."

"How long did you intend to live like this?," asked Thomas Overmann.

"I don´t know. It was clear to me that I would need a long time in order to cope with what had happened and that it would probably take several months or more than a year."

"You never heard about the so-called phantom case," said Judith Breitling.

"No, I didn´t read any newspapers and I didn´t listen to the radio because I wanted to be alone to deal with my situation. I never heard about the crimes of the alleged phantom, and of course I didn´t know that I…" Daniela paused, and the two detectives sensed that the idea of having been mistaken for a serial criminal was still inconceivable for her.

"We understand that it´s difficult for you to talk about this. We actually only want to find out how we could make such a mistake."

Daniela smiled briefly and continued: "While I was shopping, something happened once which I thought was really strange. From a distance, I overheard a conversation between the owner of the convenience store and her husband, and I heard him say: 'She looks somewhat like the phantom, doesn´t she?' His wife answered: 'Oh, Hans, I think you´re seeing things. This young woman would never hurt anyone.' I didn´t know what he meant and thought that I might have misunderstood something. That´s why I didn´t spend much time thinking about it especially since the owner of the store was friendly like she always was and even gave me free food again. Of course, it´s also possible that she didn´t recognize me because… well, body care wasn´t always so easy. I used to wash myself and my clothes in a small lake nearby, and I had to cut my hair myself. So I didn´t really look spic and span."

The two detectives laughed, and Thomas Overmann said: "You really seem to have a sense of humor. It´s clear that your appearance changed significantly. Our colleagues in the police and the criminal investigation department didn´t recognize you either based on older pictures or the composite sketch of the 'unknown female person', especially since you were in really tough shape at the end. Anyway, please continue. How did you end up in this spruce tree plantation?"

"I lived in the forest for several months and didn´t want to return to Mannheim, especially not to my mother and her boyfriend. But over time poor nutrition was taking its toll, and I knew that I wouldn´t be able to stay in the forest forever. Still, I absolutely didn´t want to return to my old life, and if I had seen Benjamin again, the wounds which had just healed would have been torn open again. So I stayed in my tent even when the nights began to get colder. Actually it worked out quite well even in the winter because I had a warm sleeping bag. But then a longer cold spell came with really icy nights, and I started to become desperate. In the end, I didn't care anymore about what was going to happen. One day, I just left without any clear goal and kept on walking even at night. I don't know anymore how I got to this spruce tree plantation. I only vaguely remember that I was becoming number and number, and then I woke up in the hospital."

"Well, you were very lucky… The doctors told us later that you only survived because of a fortunate coincidence and your extraordinarily strong constitution. If the forester hadn't found you, you probably would have died of exposure."

"What's going to happen now?," asked Daniela.

"After you've recovered, someone from the welfare office is going to come and discuss your future with you. Since you're meanwhile of age, you can ultimately make all the decisions yourself. We're also going to stay in touch with you and try to help you as much as we can," said Thomas Overmann, and Judith Breitling continued: "Thank you for answering our questions. We understand a lot of things better now and can see how some inconsistencies in this case came about."

"What do you think about this case?," Judith Breitling asked Thomas Overmann after they had said goodbye to Daniela.

"Well, it's a shocking story which shows how far removed from reality the theories about the 'phantom' were. You really have to ask yourself how this young woman could be mistaken for a cruel and violent criminal and why so many colleagues and the media believed in the existence of the 'unknown female person'."

"To be honest, this story reminds me of the fairy tale 'The Emperor's New Clothes'," said Judith Breitling. "As the phantom legend developed and found influential supporters, more and more people believed it or at least acted as if they believed it, and those who had doubts were made outsiders. At the beginning people perhaps tried to see similarities that were actually only mere coincidence. We tend to look for explanations which make our lives easier even though they often prove to be very wrong later. It would certainly have been far harder to treat all these cases as independent crimes and to investigate each one individually, especially those where we might have met with resistance or come up against bigger obstacles. After we had followed this lead for a while, it was almost impossible for our superiors and the rest of the team to admit that the theory might be wrong because we would have had to start at the beginning again. The more time we spent searching for the phantom, the more difficult it became for us to admit that we had been misled. That's why fewer and fewer people in the department doubted this theory."

"You're definitely right," said Thomas Overmann. "I'm especially amazed that the phantom myth made an entirely innocent girl who had been a victim of severe harassment a suspect."

"Her undoing was that she had become an outsider not only because of the bullying and physical attacks, but also because she defended herself. That's why many people were ready to believe and spread such a story. Of course, the ambivalent fascination for strong women plays a role. Such women have become more important in movies and novels, but many men still refuse to accept them or consider them as a threat."

"From what I've seen young men are especially fascinated by strong women when their physical strength is far exaggerated and they're portrayed as brawling and shooting heroines," said Thomas Overmann. "But this fascination also contains an element of fear which damages the self-esteem of some men and calls their superiority into question. This was reflected in the image of the phantom, a woman who had almost supernatural strength. And again, only a few wanted to contradict the widely-held belief that a person like the phantom could actually exist."

Several weeks later, Daniela was set to be discharged from the hospital, and Judith Breitling and Thomas Overmann visited her again. Meanwhile, a lot had changed for her because her fate had met with an overwhelming response from the public, who now perceived her as a victim of violence, intrigue, and incredible ignorance. Magazines were interested in her story, and a journalist planned to write a book about her experiences with her. In addition, she had already received a considerable amount of money in donations, which would allow her to rent an apartment and cover her living expenses in the coming months.

"We're glad that your life has taken such a happy turn," said Thomas Overmann. Daniela smiled and after a short while she said:

"It could have been different…"

"This is true," said Judith Breitling. "We've also come to inform you that Benjamin contacted us. He'd like to see you…" Daniela fought back the tears for a moment and answered: "Tell him that I'd be very happy if he came. I didn't really believe that we would see each other again some day."

"What are your plans for the future?," asked Judith Breitling.

"I'd like to finish high school and then maybe become a gym teacher."

"I think that's a good idea," said Thomas Overmann.

The same day in the afternoon, the members of the task force met in order to discuss the latest developments. Some cases which had been ascribed to the unknown criminal had meanwhile been solved, but numerous others were still open. And the detectives kept asking themselves how they could have made such an incredible series of mistakes. Again, they emphasized that the phantom theory was based on DNA analysis, which was solid scientific evidence. At the end of the discussion, however, Thomas Overmann addressed his colleagues and said:

"We shouldn't forget that people are manipulable. Scientific progress can't change that." Some of his colleagues nodded, but most remained silent.

TAMANRASSET

As the streetcar left the downtown area and the middle-class residential sections with their historical late 19th century houses behind it in the dusk of the slowly ending rainy day, Susanne let the last years of her life pass by. Her thoughts again revolved around her dissertation and her relationship with Christoph, whose future was as uncertain as her professional prospects. As they fleetingly said goodbye to each other on their way to the university that morning, she realized how much they had grown apart in the past months and how different their plans for the future were. While she dreamed of a career as a lecturer of philosophy, Christoph wanted to start a family at the end of his engineering practicum and possibly move to a different city or go abroad. Even though Susanne had minored in mathematics so that she would have other career options, she could hardly imagine anything else except a career at the university. Unfortunately her doctoral dissertation on "The Deconstruction of Reality in the Works of Platon, Descartes, and Derrida" had not developed as she had imagined. The more she delved into the topic, the farther she seemed to stray from her goal. As soon as she believed that she was able to follow a train of thought to the end, it turned out that she had been misled and had gone in a circle. The meeting with her supervisor today had also confirmed her feeling, but she had no idea which direction she should take in order to find a way out of this confusion.

Meanwhile, the streetcar had reached the final stop, and she walked the few steps to the two-bedroom apartment where she had been living with Christoph for four years.

As soon as she opened the door, she saw him in the living room. He asked her how the conversation with her supervisor had been.

"Unfortunately not like I would have wished," she replied. "I still have the feeling that I´m getting nowhere and that I keep following trails which don´t lead anywhere."

"Maybe you should just abandon this entire project and do something completely different," said Christoph. "You don´t absolutely have to work on the development of transmissions like I do, but you would have countless other possibilities besides this dissertation even if you did have to give up your dream of becoming a lecturer of philosophy. You know, sometimes I have a look at your books, and I have to tell you that I don´t understand some of these modern philosophers. They seem to deliberately choose a language which doesn´t say anything and at the same time can be interpreted in any possible manner. These deconstructing 'thinkers' call everything radically into question and don´t give any answers. In some of these books, there is not one single clear, binding statement and not even one conclusive line of thought based on well-defined concepts. Under these circumstances, it´s certainly no miracle that you´re not making any progress with your dissertation. As a sober engineer, I definitely like car construction better than a so-called deconstruction of reality, whatever that´s supposed to be."

"Just leave me alone," answered Susanne and went to the study. She put her briefcase next to her desk and sat down in front of the computer, unable to think clearly. Christoph´s words hurt and she felt like crying. At the same time, however, she knew that he had pronounced something that she had been thinking deep down for a long time. Perhaps it was the fact that they were growing apart that had motivated him to finally say it.

After a while, Christoph came into the study and said:

"I'm sorry. I didn't want to hurt your feelings…"

"It's all right," replied Susanne. "Maybe I just need a bit more distance from my current life. Perhaps I should take a trip far away from here, for example."

"Yes, this is true. Maybe it would take your mind off this dissertation. Why don't you see what options there are?," said Christoph and returned to the living room.

After he had closed the door behind himself, Susanne turned the computer on and began to study pictures of the Sahara. Desert landscapes had always fascinated her. In her eyes, they had something magical as if they held a secret which was not easily accessible to the mind. Over and over again, she looked at photos of dunes, oases, and mountain ranges. Their vastness made her world with its tiny paths and aberrations appear small and futile and it filled her with a calmness that she had not felt in a long time. After the images had taken effect, she looked on the internet for tour operators who offered expeditions to the Sahara. She had a hiking tour in mind which would take several weeks and lead through a region rarely visited by tourists, where she was able to gain an impression of the infinity of the desert. After a while, she found a small operator who offered trekking tours through Niger and Algeria and whose target group was travelers who wanted to "immediately experience the majestic size of the Sahara in contact with nature and far from civilization." When Christoph came back into the study, she asked him what he thought of it.

"The idea isn't bad," he replied. "Maybe it will help you to leave the 'deconstruction of reality' behind you."

"At least this trip would allow me to think a lot of things through, also with regard to our relationship. It's possible that this dissertation really won´t lead anywhere, but I still feel that there are other things in my life that matter besides efficiency, productivity, and profit."

"Whatever," said Christoph. "In any case, I´m going to the movies with my co-workers as planned. I´ll be back around midnight."

After he had left, Susanne wrote an e-mail to the tour operator asking for more detailed information. Just half an hour later, she received a reply with information material where the course of the journey was described in more depth. A small group of up to six travelers would first fly to Tamanrasset in Algeria, from where they would head to the remote oasis of Chirfa in Niger in an all-terrain vehicle. There, the hiking tour would begin, which would lead the group through the sand and stone desert past the Hoggar mountains back to Tamanrasset. During the trek, the group´s luggage would be carried by camels. The travelers themselves would walk a total of almost 500 miles through the desert in daily stretches of 15 miles. The entire tour was supposed to take approximately five weeks. It was planned that the group would spend the nights in tents or out in the open and have some rest days in oases along the way. Susanne was taken by the description immediately. When Christoph returned shortly after midnight and she told him about her idea, he only said:

"This is a real expedition. I hope that you won´t lose your way. But who knows…maybe you´ll return completely changed."

"Yes, this is well possible," answered Susanne and briefly looked into Christoph´s eyes.

The next day, she told her parents about her plans. They seemed slightly concerned because of the length of the journey through a remote region, but they knew that Susanne often went on long mountainbike and hiking tours and was therefore physically fit enough for such an expedition. And in particular they also believed that their daughter needed a change of scenery in order to leave this difficult phase of her life behind her. After a few more days of consideration, Susanne was sure that this offer was the right choice for her and registered for the trip in autumn. She would leave in mid-September and be back at the end of October in time for the beginning of the winter semester.

During the weeks prior to her flight to Algeria, Susanne kept working on her dissertation, whose completion seemed farther away than ever before. She also read books about the Sahara and gathered information about the planned travel route. The closer her journey came, the more the rugged mountains, the endless ocean of dune landscapes, and the vast starry sky untouched by the world of civilization fascinated her. When the morning of departure had finally come, she said goodbye to Christoph and got on the train to Frankfurt. He had only briefly wished her well and already seemed far away in his thoughts.

While she was waiting for the flight to Algiers at the airport, she saw a young man in the waiting area who she thought might be a member of the travel group. He was slightly taller than she was, had dark brown hair like hers and brown eyes and was carrying a backpack with a hat attached to it. Before she had a chance to talk to him, the passengers boarded the airplane, and shortly afterwards their journey from the cool late German summer to the immense expanses of the Sahara began. While they were flying over the Mediterranean coast of France, Susanne felt the tension of the past weeks, the thoughts concerning her career, and the insecurity about her relationship with Christoph receding for the first time.

Little time had passed before they landed in Algiers, where the plane to Tamanrasset was waiting. As they flew over the

Sahara, Susanne got a first impression not only of its size and beauty, but also of the mercilessness of the desert with its endless sand plains and rock formations, which she had only known from pictures so far. She saw the distant Hoggar mountains and for the first time she felt not only joy, but also a slight sensation of vulnerability in this inhospitable environment.

Upon arrival, a small group of tourists with backpacks gathered in the airport´s reception hall. Among them she recognized the young man she had already noticed in Frankfurt. It was indeed her travel group, and she was the only woman among four men. The young man smiled when he recognized her. She learned that his name was Michael and that he was studying astrophysics and working on a dissertation like her. Then she got to know the other group members. There was Martin, a 35-year old lawyer, tall, with blonde hair and blue eyes, Klaus, who was rather small, but strong with brown hair and gray-green eyes, 38 years old and by profession manager at a medium-sized company, and finally Thorsten, the travel guide, who at the age of 40 was the oldest in the group and whose suntanned face showed that he was familiar with the desert. He told the group members that a couple who had booked the journey had had to cancel at short notice. Then the bus departed for the centre of the city, which looked modern, but nevertheless left the visitors with the feeling that they had come to the edge of civilization.

In the evening, they met in the hotel´s restaurant in order to get to know each other better during their first dinner together. As could be expected, the conversation initially focused on what each of them did for a living. Susanne briefly talked about her dissertation and her plans for the future and Michael tried to explain the topic of his doctoral thesis on supernovae, which he had begun a year ago. Martin gave an account of his job as a defense attorney and expressly mentioned that he had appeared in some spectacular murder cases. Not surprisingly, Thorsten was quite sure that he had already read Martin's name in the newspaper. Klaus only briefly described his work as head of personnel at a large advertising agency. Then he related stories from his mountaineering tours, which had led him into the Alps and once even to an 18,000-foot summit in the Himalayas. Afterwards, he asked Thorsten about his experiences as a travel guide. Thorsten replied that he had been guiding tourists through the Sahara for more than six years and that, among other things, he had previously been in charge of trekking tours in the Himalayas. This was the beginning of a long, lively conversation between Klaus and Thorsten about their hiking tours and mountaineering expeditions, the highest peaks of the Earth, and the ways of climbing them. Martin was listening almost in a trance while Susanne and Michael were finding out more about each other's research. Susanne tried to explain the topic of her dissertation as well as possible and told Michael about her difficulties.

"Sometimes, I also have the feeling that I've come to a dead end even though my topic is far clearer and more concrete than yours. Once, it also happened that the results of the experiments did not match the theory and I had to start from scratch again while I was in the middle of a chapter. Therefore I can imagine how you feel now," said Michael.

"Thank you. I haven't experienced so much understanding in a long time," answered Susanne happily. She was relieved because she had expected that as a scientist Michael would show little appreciation for her work.

At the end of the meal, the group drank to an exciting journey over a glass of wine before returning to their rooms. All were eager to get a good night's rest because they knew that they would have to get up early the next morning as the plan was to cover more than half of the way to Chirfa.

Early in the morning, they loaded the all-terrain vehicle with their tents and backpacks and set off on their journey. The ride to Chirfa was scheduled to take almost two days. Soon the last houses of the city were behind them. For the first time, they saw the desert with its boulder-strewn plains and sand fields, above which the peaks of the Hoggar mountains towered from afar. They encountered quite a few cars and trucks on the road and saw some camel caravans in the distance. At the beginning they did not at all feel isolated in the vastness of the Sahara, but the greater the distance from Tamanrasset, the fewer people they met in the shadeless sea of sand and rocks. Their ride led them through plains full of dunes, across mountains and valleys, and past narrow ravines which, as it seemed, nobody had ever entered and whose ground disappeared from the bright light of the afternoon sunshine into an impenetrable darkness.

When they left the road at dusk to set up their tents in a small valley near a group of withered acacias, they became aware of how far away this landscape was from their lives in Europe. Thorsten brought some firewood, and the small group sat around the campfire as the heat of the day gave way to a penetrating cold, which made them shiver in this same place that was so scorchingly hot during the day. No one talked much. They were all too busy digesting their new experiences and getting used to the unexpected cold of the early night.

After the others had retreated to their tents, Susanne observed the sky. In the dry desert air, countless stars and the wide ribbon of the Milky Way appeared more clearly than ever before in Germany. The calmness of the starry sky made her forget the cold of the nightly desert until she finally spread her sleeping bag in front of her tent and tried to sleep until the morning.

The next day they continued their ride until they finally reached Chirfa, a small oasis in the middle of a sand desert characterized by a mix of dunes and rocks. The oasis itself consisted of a group of smaller, bright mud brick houses surrounded by a palm grove, where Thorsten refilled their water containers at a well. On this occasion, the members of the travel group noticed that he spoke the language of the locals fluently, who were observing the tourists with reserved curiosity even though European travelers stopped in Chirfa quite frequently. When Susanne asked Thorsten about his language skills, he told her that he had learned the language of the Tuareg and other tongues since he spent time in this region constantly and that he knew this part of the Sahara, the Ténéré, so well that he was able to lead travel groups even without the help of local guides.

Early the next day, the two pack camels which were going to carry the luggage, food, and water containers were loaded. The water cans and food reserves would be refilled in oases and wells along the way, allowing the group to trek through the almost uninhabited desert for several weeks. They planned to cover a considerable part of the first day´s stretch before the heat became unbearable at noontime. Their path led them northwest through sand dunes and boulder-strewn plains while the warmth of the beginning day was driving away the cold of the night. After several hours, as the sun was approaching the zenith and the air and the sand were absorbing more and more heat, the group took its first break in the shade of a dune. The travelers thoughtfully observed the endless landscape while quenching their thirst with water and tea. The scenery made a powerful impression on Susanne, but she also felt an immediate sensation of threat and isolation in the middle of the desert. Despite her admiration for the beauty of nature, she asked herself what the Sahara would be like without water, but she quickly pushed the thought aside when the others began walking again.

In the afternoon, they reached the next rest area which was under a ledge in a small valley with a view of an immense landscape sprinkled with bluish-black rocks. It seemed endless, and if they had not reminded themselves that the Earth was round, they would have believed that there were no boundaries to what they saw. Almost three hours had passed when the worst afternoon heat subsided and they began the third leg of their journey, which would end at their first campsite. Their route led them out of the boulder-strewn plain into a dune landscape. At the end of this area of dunes, a hilly region appeared in whose direction they intended to set out on the next day.

At the end of a cool night, they continued their way across the dunes and a treeless plain. In the afternoon, they reached the hilly region where the boulders of a valley hid prehistoric petroglyphs which Thorsten was familiar with from previous expeditions. After a short climb from the bottom of the valley, they were able to see the paintings of cattle and hunters on reddish sandstone and caught a glimpse of a distant past. Filled with awe, they descended back down into the valley and walked several miles until they reached their next campsite on a small high plateau.

When the sun had already set and the last shimmer of dusk was illuminating the sky, the weary travelers, now content following a good meal, sat around the campfire. Lively conversations began to develop between individuals. Susanne told Michael about her budding fascination for the starry sky. While he was attempting to explain the constellations and the structure of the Milky Way to her, they were interrupted by a loud, angry discussion between Martin and Klaus, which continued to rise in volume.

"Freedom is the greatest asset in a constitutional state and more important than anything else," said Martin.

"Freedom, however, also means responsibility and, above all, the obligation of the individual to care for himself," answered Klaus.

"But if someone is not able to lead a materially secure life, he is entitled to help from the community without any restrictions on his freedom."

"Nonetheless, comprehensive public welfare always means limitation of individual freedom and growing power of the government."

"Restrictions on freedom are unacceptable in all circumstances including when someone is entitled to welfare payments, and even if people break laws every limitation of freedom has to be viewed with the greatest suspicion."

During a short moment of silence, Susanne said:

"Doesn't unlimited freedom of the individual ultimately lead to the survival of the fittest, which means that the rights and the freedom of those who are weaker are disregarded?" Neither seemed to know what to answer to this objection and only briefly and blankly looked at Susanne before continuing their discussion. Michael and Susanne got up and climbed onto a small dune several hundred yards away from their campsite.

"This entire argument about freedom is somewhat strange," said Susanne. "In the past, when I was in school, I still had teachers who were marked by the hippie era and who were all enthusiastic about creating a new individual more capable of life in the community and who bombarded us with the related psychological theories. As a teenager, I protested against these ideas and sometimes had quite heated arguments with these teachers. But today only exaggerated individualism and the pursuit of unlimited freedom seem to count, at least for those people who feel strong and believe that they belong to the winners."

"Once, I read a clever saying somewhere. I just don't remember who it was from. It said, 'One must only become old enough to experience everything and the opposite of everything' ," replied Michael.

"Well, then we certainly still have a lot ahead of us," said Susanne.

"If we're not swallowed by the desert before…," replied Michael, and they both laughed. They gazed silently at the starry sky for a while and then returned to their campsite. As they lay down to sleep, they briefly heard the argument between Klaus and Martin becoming more and more violent and noisy before it suddenly ended and only the silence of the clear night surrounded the group.

The following day, they continued to hike through the hilly region where the mountains slowly became higher and the valleys became deeper. Late in the afternoon, they reached another small plateau between two valleys, of which one narrowed into a ravine in the distance. After they had lit their campfire and eaten dinner, Thorsten said:

"I'd like to have a closer look at the valley back there. Locals have told me that there is a cave with particularly beautiful petroglyphs. Don't worry about me if I'm back late. You know that I'm familiar with the Sahara."

"We have no doubts that you won't get lost," answered Klaus. "Somebody who is able to climb on Himalayan summits shouldn't have any difficulties in this valley."

Thorsten said goodbye to the others and put his backpack on, in which he carried his satellite navigator along with other equipment. Several minutes later, the travelers saw Thorsten walking in the direction of the narrowing valley. After a while they watched him disappear between two dunes, just a dot which was gradually becoming smaller. The sun was still shining, but it was slowly approaching the horizon.

"I hope that he'll be back before darkness falls and that it won't rain," said Susanne and pointed at a distant cloud formation.

"It's not looking like rain, and even if it rains, the drops often don't even reach the ground in the Sahara. In addition, Thorsten knows what he's doing and would find his way even in the dark especially since he has his satellite navigator with him," answered Martin.

The group sat around the campfire for a while longer until Martin went into his tent. Susanne and Michael left for a little walk as on the day before. She told him more about the problems with her dissertation and said:

"The longer I work on it, the more I have the impression that the approach is questionable even though it's currently considered very promising and something like the ultimate. My adviser once said quoting a colleague that it was pointless to just simply spit into a large river, but…"

"Sometimes it's better to spit into a river than to swim along in it," replied Michael.

"Yes," said Susanne and laughed. "We ultimately have to find our own way even if we have to leave the beaten path and question apparent certainties."

Suddenly, they heard a loud bang and were unsure where it had come from.

"What was that?," asked Susanne.

"Maybe thunder," replied Michael.

"Strange. We didn't see any lightning."

At that moment, they heard the loud, eerie noise twice more.

"Come, it's time for us to return to our tents," said Susanne.

When they reached their campsite, Klaus was still awake and answered in response to their question that Thorsten had not yet returned.

"Did you also hear that noise?," asked Susanne.

"Yes, of course."

"What could it have been?," asked Michael.

"No idea," said Klaus. "Maybe a thunderstorm. Even in the desert, there are thunderstorms at times."

"I hope that Thorsten is all right," said Susanne.

"Don't worry," replied Klaus. "He knows the region and has already traveled in alpine environments, where people often have to cope with sudden weather changes and unforeseen events. I have no doubts that he's fine. We'd only have to look for him if he weren't back by tomorrow morning."

Susanne and Michael did not say anything because they knew that it would be impossible to find Thorsten in the completely dark and entirely unknown environment. All four decided to get some sleep and to wait until morning. Susanne slept only little during the night and was already awake at the break of dawn. She and her three fellow travelers noticed immediately that Thorsten still had not returned, something which Susanne and Michael had feared. The little group decided to search for its guide and, without taking the time for breakfast, headed in the direction of the valley which Thorsten had wanted to explore. After approximately an hour, they reached the valley entrance. The deeper they penetrated into this valley, the taller and narrower its rocky walls became, in which numerous cave entrances were visible. In addition, many small canyons branched off the main valley, which seemed to form a large labyrinth.

"It will be difficult to find Thorsten in this maze of side valleys, caves, and rocky walls," said Susanne.

"Yes, but he must be around here somewhere, and we should at least find some footprints," answered Klaus. They continued searching and walked deeper and deeper into the valley. Just as Klaus and Martin were about ready to give up, Michael suddenly saw impressions in the sand in the distance.

"There's something over there, but I don't know exactly what it is," he said.

"All right, let's have a look," said Martin. When they reached the area in question, they were taken aback and frightened by what they saw.

"These tracks look like tire prints," said Klaus.

"Yes, but I've never seen such tire tracks. They're far larger than the prints from normal tires, and I've never seen such tires even on larger trucks. In addition, the sand was compressed under a heavy weight. Look, it almost seems petrified in some spots," said Martin. After short deliberation, the group followed the tire tracks and saw that they ended at the entrance of a side valley.

"This is strange," said Michael.

"True. But one explanation would be that the wind from the canyon has blown them over. Maybe we should look for other prints in this side valley," replied Susanne. Klaus and Martin only reluctantly agreed with the proposal, but even they saw hardly any other way to find Thorsten. After they had explored the narrow side valley for more than three hours, they decided to head back in the direction they had come from as they had not discovered even one single trace of Thorsten. When they reached the point where the canyon began, Klaus said:

"The only other possibility is that he went in the other direction."

Their efforts proved fruitless, however. The search for footprints was futile. Meanwhile the bottom of the valley already lay in dark shadows and the bewildered travelers decided to return to the campsite in the late afternoon as they feared that darkness might come unexpectedly and they would not be able to find their way in the labyrinth of valleys having no satellite navigators. On the way back, almost no one said a word. They were all absorbed in their own thoughts and worries. They knew that not one them had a satellite navigator, a compass, or a good map and that it would be difficult for them to find their way to Tamanrasset or even to the nearest oasis without Thorsten. When they reached the campsite, it was pitch dark. Even though they had been walking all day, they were not very hungry and soon went into their tents. They all hoped deep down that Thorsten would still find his way back even though they knew that this was very unlikely. Everyone awoke early the next morning after a night of little rest and began to discuss the situation while sitting around a scant fire.

"What could have happened to Thorsten?," asked Susanne.

"Well, he could have been surprised by a thunderstorm," said Klaus. "Sometimes, there are sudden downpours in the Sahara which cause flash floods. Such a flood could have surprised him, and he could have fled to a higher cave."

"But the tracks in the sand don´t match this theory," objected Martin. "In addition, we didn´t see any signs of flood or flowing water."

"What does everyone think about these strange tire prints?," asked Susanne.

"I´ve never seen such tracks before, and they don´t match any vehicles that I know," replied Klaus.

"Maybe Thorsten was attacked or kidnapped by a gang of smugglers or terrorists, for example. You know that this region is sometimes haunted by such people," said Michael.

"What kinds of terrorists or smugglers use vehicles with such gigantic tires?," asked Martin angrily. "You could almost believe that something fishy is going on here. Who knows what happened to Thorsten? Maybe…"

Susanne interrupted him and tried to stay as calm as possible even though she also felt extremely uneasy.

"There´s an explanation for everything, and I mean a natural and rational one even if we don´t know what it is. It doesn´t make sense to keep speculating about what could have happened to Thorsten. The decisive question is, what are we going to do now?"

"Do you have any ideas?," asked Martin furiously.

"The problem is that we have water for no more than four to five days. This means that we have to find either the nearest oasis or the road to Tamanrasset as quickly as possible," said Susanne.

"And what about Thorsten?," asked Klaus.

"If we die of thirst, we definitely won't be able to help him. The only thing we can do is to get help as fast as possible," answered Michael.

"Then it would be best if we looked for the road to Tamanrasset. I have a little map with me. It isn't very good, but I can rely on my sense of direction. We could reach the road within a maximum of two days..."

"No," said Martin, interrupting him. "We first need water. In order to find the way to the nearest oasis, we only have to keep walking straight ahead. I guess you'll be able to manage that."

"Unfortunately, it's not that easy," said Michael. "If people try to walk straight ahead without having set control points, they often go in circles. I think that we should use the course of the sun during the day and the stars at night for orientation and try to find the road to Tamanrasset. We know its approximate location, whereas we don't know where the oasis is."

"Quit talking nonsense, little boy!," Martin yelled seething with anger. "You don't mean to imply that I'm not able to walk straight ahead properly? Maybe you're incapable of doing that because you spend all day at a desk, but I can manage it."

Susanne was alarmed by his aggressiveness and tried to calm him by responding to his proposal.

"Maybe we could try to reach the oasis within one day. This should be possible if we hurry and walk until late at night. From there, the road to Tamanrasset should actually also be closer. If we have the impression that we're losing our way or if we don't arrive by tomorrow morning, we could look for a different route."

Michael supported Susanne's proposal as he thought it best to avoid further confrontation with Martin. Klaus agreed reluctantly, but only under the condition that the others would follow his plan if they did not reach the oasis by the next day. This implication immediately caused a violent eruption from Martin, but the matter had finally been settled.

They set out with the two pack camels later in the morning. The only thing they knew about the oasis was that it was one to two days away at normal speed. Martin guided the little group and tried to continue the route previously taken by Thorsten. Walking across the dunes and through the deep sand became more and more arduous as a strong wind started to stir up the sand towards midday. It penetrated into their clothes, stuck to their moist, sweaty skin, and immerged the desert in a diffuse, dim light, which made orientation more difficult. In the early afternoon, they sat around a small campfire and tried to gather new strength during a short break before they continued their way into the unknown. Later in the afternoon, the wind became slightly stronger and grains of sand formed a reddish fog in which all outlines became blurred. Towards the evening, they finally reached a point on the summit of a dune which seemed familiar to them. After a while, there was no doubt that they had walked in a circle just as Michael had feared. The oasis was as far away as it had been in the morning, and all pain and effort of the day had been in vain. Susanne and Michael began to feel despair even though they had suspected that something like this would happen. Martin and Klaus, however, immediately became involved in a violent dispute.

"It's true, we went in a circle," said Klaus angrily.

"It's not my fault if the weather is bad. In addition, we would have walked in a circle even if we had followed your foolish plan to look for the road to Tamanrasset," Martin shouted.

"Why foolish?," asked Klaus. "It was your proposal that was foolish as you can see now."

"What?," yelled Martin furiously. "You and our two young graduate students only want to play the know-it-alls, but you don´t have the faintest idea." As the quarrel between the two continued to escalate, Susanne said to Michael:

"Sometimes, I almost fear our fellow travelers more than the desert and what´s hidden in it."

"I feel the same," replied Michael. "They like to talk about freedom, but ultimately they only care about themselves."

While they were talking, they saw that Martin had grabbed Klaus by the collar and tried to knock him down. However, Klaus tore himself free and slammed his fist into Martin´s face twice. Martin fell and lay on the ground for several moments before he picked himself back up. His nose was bleeding, and his left eye was swollen.

"You´ll pay for that!," he yelled and began to set his tent up, where he sought shelter briefly afterwards.

Susanne and Michael tried to calm Klaus before they began to prepare for the night. The wind had died down, and an almost supernatural serenity lay over the desert. In the twilight. the stars began to shine in the sky. In their light the desert appeared as if it did not belong to this world and were part of eternity. Susanne and Michael quietly observed the firmament for a long time before they also lay down to sleep. After Susanne had been asleep for several hours, she was awoken by a noise which she believed was similar to the bang that they had heard the night Thorsten had disappeared. She sat up, and after approximately two minutes she saw a red glow on the horizon like the distant illumination of a deadly, blazing dawn. After a few seconds it was followed by deep, growling thunder. Michael had also woken up, and Susanne asked in a frightened voice:

"My God, what is that?"

"I don´t know either," said Michael. "In any case, we´re back near the valley which Thorsten wanted to explore."

"Tomorrow, we have to leave here as quickly as possible."

"Yes, but before we should try to sleep a little in order to regain our strength."

Both lay back down, but they fell asleep only in the early morning for one or two hours. When they woke up, Klaus was already up, but Martin´s tent looked as if he were still sleeping in it. Only after no one had stirred for about half an hour did Susanne decide to check. She opened the canvas cover to the entrance and saw that Martin was not there. His sleeping bag and his backpack were gone as well, and soon afterwards the travelers noticed that some water containers and some of the provisions were also missing. Obviously, Martin had left the group during the night in order to travel his own route.

"We have to try to find him and convince him not to walk on alone," said Susanne.

"But how can we do that?," asked Klaus. "His footprints have meanwhile been almost completely covered by drifting sand. In addition, we don´t know which direction he could have taken."

"Did you also hear that noise again last night?," asked Susanne.

"I think that I heard something once while I was half asleep, but I drifted back into a deep sleep immediately," replied Klaus. Susanne told him that she and Michael had heard the strange thunder again in the middle of the night.

"Then we absolutely shouldn´t return to this valley," said Klaus.

"I agree with you," answered Michael. "We also can´t forget that we have only little water and few provisions left."

"We have to look for the road to Tamanrasset," said Klaus and took a small map out of his backpack. "At the moment, we are approximately here, which means that we have to head south-west. That′s over there."

"This should be more or less the right direction," said Michael.

"Then let′s go," replied Klaus.

The three packed their bags and left in order to take advantage of the calm weather before it possibly changed again. While they were trekking across dunes and boulder-strewn plains, they tried not to drink too much despite the growing heat. Although they feared dehydration, they knew that their water supplies were limited. As they were crossing a virtually endless plain full of boulders and bizarre rocks, Susanne was overpowered by an increasing, burning sensation in her mouth and her throat, which made speaking and swallowing a torture. She felt a throbbing and hammering pain in her head, which paralyzed her thoughts until they gave way to a feeling of extreme lightheadedness. Nothing mattered to her except the next drink of water, the needs of her tormented body, and her nightmares. In the glaring sunlight of the treeless plain, the black rocks began mutating into dark remnants of a distant past, into fabulous sphinx-like creatures, snakes, and monsters, which held her spellbound until she finally awoke from her trance-like state and tried not to let the frightening images overwhelm her any longer.

Soon they reached a large boulder, in whose shadow they had a long rest, and decided to wait until the most intense midday heat had passed. Klaus was convinced that they were going the right way, and Michael, who had tried to use the position and the course of the sun for orientation, believed and hoped that he was right. Two hours later they continued their trek until they finally reached a sandy area where large dunes cast shadows and offered some relief from the heat. At night, they set up their campsite at the foot of one of these dunes and soon fell into a deep sleep, from which Susanne woke up once with a start because she thought that she had heard distant thunder and seen a glowing light. She was not sure if it had been a nightmare or reality. While she was awake, however, everything remained silent, and she soon drifted back to sleep until the early morning.

The next day they continued walking as the sun slowly rose and the dunes gave way to a stone desert. After several hours, Klaus stopped abruptly.

"Look! There's something over there. It looks like an oasis."

"No, I think it's just the shimmering of the air in the heat," said Susanne. "I'm sure that it's an oasis. I see water, palm trees, and a road with traveling cars," answered Klaus, "We absolutely have to replenish our water supplies there."

"We shouldn't do that," said Susanne. "It's a mirage."

Michael nodded and said:

"We can't allow ourselves to be deceived by this vision under any circumstances. This could be a deadly mistake."

"You pampered intellectuals have no idea!," screamed Klaus furiously. "There, Martin was entirely right. I'm taking the two camels now to get more water in the oasis." Susanne thought for a moment and said:

"Let the two of us at least fill our water bottles beforehand."

"You don't believe me and think that you know everything better," replied Klaus full of contempt.

"No, we don't know everything better, but we've gone the wrong way once before and we don't want to die in the desert," said Susanne and looked Klaus firmly in the eyes.

"We're going to fill our water bottles now. Then you can do whatever you want," added Michael and began to fill the bottles with water from the containers, where most of the water supply remained when he was finished. Finally, Klaus snatched the container out of Michael's hand and roared:

"I've had enough!"

He put it back and wandered away without saying a word. Susanne and Michael watched him until he disappeared from view in the flimmering air of the horizon.

"What are we going to do now?," asked Michael.

"I think we should wait until tomorrow and see whether he comes back. If not, we're going to look for him, and if we don't find him, we have to walk on."

Michael agreed with Susanne. They waited for hours in the shade of a crippled tree nearby as dusk slowly fell. They only rarely sipped water from their bottles and were at first silently engrossed in their thoughts. Gradually, they yielded to their growing indifference and drowsiness and neither awoke until the next day.

"Michael," said Susanne when she woke up, "Klaus isn't back yet. It's time for us to look for him."

"You're right," answered Michael. His strength also seemed to have returned.

They began their search for Klaus by heading in the direction he had taken. At several places they found footprints which helped them. These ended abruptly at the beginning of a boulder-strewn area, however. After a short moment of reflection, they both decided to walk on straight ahead. Several hundred yards away, they saw a figure lying on the ground. They knew immediately that it had to be Klaus. He lay there motionless and bent, and when they got closer they noticed that his face was distorted by pain and appeared to be frozen. The two camels were nowhere to be seen. Susanne felt for a pulse, but she was not able to detect any heartbeat or any respiration, and neither was Michael.

"My God, he's dead. What could have happened to him?"

"Maybe he died of thirst or a heatstroke," answered Michael while he was examining Klaus' body more closely. Then he saw two red spots near the right ankle.

"These could be scorpion bites," he said. "Some of the most poisonous scorpion species in the world live in this region of the Sahara."

"Yes, you're right. That could be the reason for his death. My God, this is probably the third casualty within three days. Whatever we do now, we've got to stick together," said Susanne.

"Right. We all should have done that before, but I think that at least the two of us agree on what to do now," replied Michael.

"Yes. We'll follow your plan and try to use the stars for orientation. How much water is left?"

"I have approximately four liters, and there are about five liters in your backpack. That should be enough for almost two days if we use it sparingly. We have to try to walk on as long as possible at night after sunset and leave in the morning before the sun rises."

"Do you think that we'll find the way?," asked Susanne.

"I can't make any promises, but I know the constellations really well. At least I can halfway determine the direction."

"Then let's try it. We have nothing to lose," replied Susanne.

"Do you believe in God?," asked Michael suddenly.

"To be honest, I'm not really religious, but I've sometimes asked myself especially here in the isolation of the desert if there might be something else beyond the material world we live in, which is so important in our wealth-oriented societies. It's a great mystery to me ... ," answered Susanne.

"Maybe it's like with the stars. They're full of mysteries and can nevertheless give us an idea of where the right way might be even if we ultimately have to find it ourselves," said Michael. Susanne briefly looked at him and replied:

"Wherever our way will take us, at least we won't walk and die alone like Klaus and probably Thorsten and Martin," said Susanne. Michael answered with a brief smile before they departed into the night following the setting sun in the direction in which they believed they would find the road to Tamanrasset. Susanne watched the starry sky intently again as she had at their first campsite at the beginning of the journey, but this time the glowing of the stars and their distant white light gave her an even stronger impression of being a tiny grain of sand in infinity, which made her feel lost and nonetheless gave her a feeling of security. Michael knew all the constellations precisely, and Susanne sensed that despite their threatening situation they were heading the right way. After they had walked in silence for a while, she began to ask him questions about the world of the stars, and he explained the structure of the starry sky and the cosmos as well as the life cycle of the stars.

"Then it's true that we're ultimately all stardust," said Susanne.

"In a certain way yes," replied Michael.

"I was never interested in all this before even though it might have more to do with the deepest questions of life than some philosophical theories," said Susanne.

"Yes, sometimes astronomers pursue such thoughts, too," said Michael. "Maybe astronomy and philosophy really do have more in common than people think."

After they had walked through the nightly desert for several hours, they rested at the foot of a dune for some time before they continued their way until the sun rose and the coolness of the night gave way to the heat of the day. Their water supply had meanwhile dwindled to five liters, and they both knew that they did not have much time left. During the day, they tried to get some sleep in the shadow of a dune, although the sun, the heat, and an increasingly tormenting feeling of thirst hardly allowed them to rest. Towards the evening, they began to walk again, but they had the feeling that despite all efforts they had not moved from the same spot and thought that the desert would never end no matter how far they went.

On the morning of the following day, the last water was used up, and they decided to continue on despite the rising temperatures. They knew that they only had hours or at most a day to reach their goal. As they headed into the unknown, they did not talk much, but nevertheless felt very close to each other in the face of death before the feeling of dull numbness, which they already knew so well, took possession of them shortly afterwards and this time more fiercely than ever before. Soon, they were no longer able to think of anything else but the horrible burning in their throats and the fiery heat on their skin, which grew into a gnawing pain during the coming hours. They did not notice that the landscape had begun to change and that boulder-strewn plains and sand fields were slowly taking the place of the sand desert's dunes. In the early afternoon, Susanne was close to total exhaustion and felt that she would not hold out much longer. She was convinced that she was in the middle of a blazing fire. Her head was throbbing furiously, which nearly robbed her of her last hope and made death almost seem a relief. At times, the sun's brilliance gave way to pitch darkness before her eyes, and in the depths of her soul she hoped that this darkness would soon envelop her entirely. Suddenly she heard a voice which she was not consciously aware of at first until Michael shook her out of her daze:

"Look, Susanne! I see something on the horizon. Please don't give up now. I think we're almost there." Susanne was only able to nod faintly in response, and Michael felt that he would have to gather all his strength in order to prevent her from falling over dead. He put his arm around her shoulders and slowly walked on with her expending the last of his energy. He was almost sure that they had reached their goal because he saw little moving dots in the distance behind which sand plumes rose. Despite the midday heat, he was convinced that it was not a mirage. Time seemed to stand still for him before it slowly became clear that the road he had seen was not an illusion. Susanne only faintly took notice of her environment, but nevertheless she also felt a vague sense of hope despite being half unconscious and in a state between life and death. It was not until they reached the road to Tamanrasset after more than an hour that she entirely lost consciousness. Michael knew that there was no time to lose and that Susanne urgently needed water and medical help in order to survive. Fortunately, he did not have to wait long because an all-terrain vehicle stopped after just a few minutes. In it sat a Tuareg family on their way to Tamanrasset. Michael tried to tell the father in English what had happened to them, and the two of them pooled their efforts to lift Susanne into the car before they sped off towards the city, which was still several hundred miles away. During the ride, the man asked Michael about their ordeal. When Michael told him what had happened, he noticed that he grew very silent and was hardly able to hide his fear. Michael had the impression that he knew or suspected something, but believed that it was better not to talk about it. During their conversation, his wife and their 16-year old daughter tried to pour water into Susanne´s mouth whenever she briefly regained consciousness.

Late in the evening, they finally reached Tamanrasset, where they immediately took Susanne to a hospital. The physicians told Michael that she was severely dehydrated and needed infusions, but that her situation was no longer life-threatening.

The next morning Michael went to a police station and gave the police officers an account of the events during their journey. The policemen recorded his statements and promised that they would notify the German embassy. In addition, they asked him to remain available during the following days in order to answer any questions they might have. Once again, Michael had the impression that the police, like other locals, knew or at least suspected things, but that they tried to hide this knowledge behind a wall of distant politeness and indifference.

In the afternoon, he received a visit from a representative of the German embassy who asked Michael to give him a detailed report and promised to inform the Foreign Office as quickly as possible so that the necessary measures could be taken.

When Michael visited Susanne in the hospital that evening, she had already recovered to a point where she was able to talk to him briefly. He promised her that he would not leave until she was discharged from the hospital and that they would return to Germany together.

Meanwhile, the search for Thorsten, Martin, and Klaus had already begun. It remained unsuccessful during the following days. All three seemed to have disappeared from Earth without a trace, and there were no new developments by the time Michael and Susanne were ready to return to Germany three days later. They had both been extensively questioned by the police again and had tried to indicate the geographic position of the valley where Thorsten and Martin had disappeared as precisely as possible. However, they were only able to take a guess at the approximate location since Thorsten had been the only one with a satellite navigator and therefore the only one who knew their exact position. Susanne and Michael had the impression that the police tried to conceal knowledge or suspicions, but they were glad that at least they did not seem to mistrust them and that they would be able to return to Germany without any problems.

As they waited for their flight to Algiers at the airport of Tamanrasset, where they had got to know each other almost two weeks before, they began to think about the future and the impact their ordeal had had on them.

"These last days deeply changed me," said Susanne. "The encounter with death has shown me how important it is that I go my own way and that I do what I think is best."

"Are you going to finish your dissertation?," asked Michael.

"No, I don´t think so," answered Susanne. "After what I experienced, these academic discussions seem almost trivial to me. I think that I´m going to do something totally different."

"Like what?"

"I don´t know yet exactly, but probably nothing in the area of philosophy."

"At the moment, there are two vacancies for mathematicians at our institute. If you want, you can think about an application…," said Michael. "Yes, I´m certainly going to do that," answered Susanne. "Do you still remember our conversation in the desert several days ago? I really had the impression that the desert and the view of the nightly sky brought me closer to the world´s deepest secrets than philosophical seminars."

"I often have this feeling, too," said Michael. "Even though astronomy is a sober science, I can´t resist the fascination of the sky either. And like you, I sometimes ask myself whether there is something behind all this scientifically comprehensible physical reality."

When the plane took off soon afterwards and Susanne again saw the desert from above, she remembered her arrival almost two weeks before, and this look back made her even more aware of how deeply this short, but decisive time had changed her life forever. It almost seemed to her as if part of her was gone and something new had taken its place.

After arriving in Frankfurt, she said goodbye to Michael who hugged her briefly and promised him that she would contact him soon and think about an application for a position at his institute.

As she sat in the streetcar heading to her apartment several hours later, it seemed impossible to her that she could return to her old life. Only at that moment did she fully realize that she had never felt the urge to call Christoph in the past days to tell him about her ordeal and that she was on her way home. She gaped in surprise after opening the door to her apartment. Christoph´s furniture was gone and on the kitchen table was a letter in which he told her that he had moved out because he could no longer imagine a common future with her and wanted to live with a woman he had met a short time ago. At first, Susanne was slightly perplexed, but not really shocked by the end of their relationship. It had been foreseeable given the developments of the past months. She decided to let several days pass before she made a decision about her future.

The next week went by with a visit to her parents´ house and conversations with friends whom she told her story to and whom she asked for advice. After several days, she finally sent an application to the institute of astronomy where Michael worked and received an invitation for a job interview a little later. Then she informed her adviser that she did not want to continue to work on her dissertation since she had serious doubts about the topic originally chosen.

Meanwhile, the Foreign Office had tried to find out what had happened to her three travel companions and whether Thorsten and Martin were still alive. Cooperation with the local police proved difficult, especially since Michael and Susanne were only able to provide very vague information about the positions where the three had disappeared. The media also devoted extensive reports to the topic and developed various theories about what could have happened to Thorsten and Martin. Ultimately, however, all their investigations were inconclusive. Several assumptions were made about where and in which valley the two had disappeared, but no concrete traces were found.

In newspaper and television reports, smugglers or terrorists, sudden downpours and floods, or entirely different, partially outlandish reasons for Thorsten's and Martin's disappearance were discussed, but in the end none of these theories seemed really credible. In their interrogations, Michael and Susanne themselves were not able to contribute any more to police investigations because the incidents remained puzzling, even to them.

When Susanne went to her job interview a few weeks later, she saw Michael for the first time after their journey. They both immediately felt a deep emotional bond, which had already begun to develop during their time in the Sahara. Directly after the job interview, Susanne was told that she had been granted the position, and she and Michael were thrilled about working together in the future and seeing each other daily.

Klaus was finally declared dead based on Michael's and Susanne's statements. Thorsten and Martin fell into oblivion over time. Their fate was never clarified.